MacArthur MS.

Into the
Candlelit Room

Into the Candlelit Room

AND OTHER STRANGE TALES

THOMAS McKEAN

G. P. PUTNAM'S SONS

NEW YORK

G. P. Putnam's Sons, a division of Penguin Putnam Books for Young Readers,
345 Hudson Street, New York, NY 10014

G. P. Putnam's Sons, Reg. U.S. Pat. & Tm. Off.

Published simultaneously in Canada

Printed in the United States of America

Designed by Donna Mark. Text set in Columbus

Interior art by Thomas McKean.

Library of Congress Cataloging-in-Publication Data

McKean, Thomas. Into the candlelit room / Thomas McKean. p. cm.

Summary: In a series of letters and diary entries, five young people
describe their experiences with evil and the supernatural,
including encounters with a demon, a ghost, and a fortuneteller.

[1. Demonology—Fiction.   2. Supernatural—Fiction.

3. Letters—Fiction.   4. Diaries—Fiction.]   I. Title.

PZ7.M19417In   1999   [Fic]—dc21 98-13070   CIP AC

ISBN 0-399-23359-8

1   3   5   7   9   10   8   6   4   2

FIRST IMPRESSION

For Martha S. Smith

CONTENTS

INTO THE CANDLELIT ROOM

FROM THE DIARY OF
VLADIMIR MIKULA

'm stuck here until he comes, so I might as well write in my diary. What a waste of a sunny Saturday, to be trapped here in this basement, hot as hell, waiting for some snob to show up and boss me around. I hate this apartment, but supers always get the worst apartment in the entire building. It's a law, I think. I wish my father would get a better job. I wouldn't care what it was—he could collect garbage, give traffic tickets, anything.

But being a building superintendent seems to be the only thing my father can do, at least that's what he always tells me whenever I bring it up. And if I bring it up too often, he hits me. Not hard, but hard enough. I know Grand tells him not to hit me, that Mother wouldn't have liked it—not that he listens to Grand all that much. After all, she's not *his* mother, just his mother-in-law. Grand tells me to try to take it as a sign he loves me. Right. I don't call that love. And I don't call this life, living here in this sunless, stuffy apartment, crammed into four tiny rooms. Sometimes I wish I could live with Grand instead, but her apartment's even smaller. So I'm stuck here. "It's such a nice neighborhood," someone's always reminding me, "right on Gramercy Park." Great. That just means when I go for walks I can look in fancy store windows at things I can't afford. And when I'm at school, I get to be teased by all the kids whose parents can afford to live in this neighborhood without being building superintendents. I only get to go to my school because they have a limited amount of scholarships for poor kids who live in the area. Really limited. Two— Juan Rodriguez and me.

School starts up again next week. I might actually like it a bit, if it weren't for all the rich kids who go there. They're almost all rich in my school—and I mean rich with enormous apartments and servants and summer houses on Long Island Sound or in the Adirondacks or the Catskills or some stupid place I'll never get to go. *Their* fathers are doctors or lawyers or advertising executives. *Their* mothers show up at school in limos, wearing diamonds and pearls and fancy black dresses. *My* mother is dead. And *my* father can barely speak English. If something's complicated, I have to translate it into Polish. He can't even begin to read English, so at least I can blow off steam by writing whatever I want in this diary—Grand says I've got a lot of steam to blow off. Maybe that's why she gave me this old notebook to use as a diary. Anyway, my father wouldn't be able to read this. If he even cared. He's not much on reading to start with, even in Polish. I guess he's always going to be just a super: he can't speak English well and he's good at fixing things. I'm always amazed how those big clumsy hands can do such fine repair work—plumbing, electrical, whatever. I just don't see why he has to hit me with them. He's big, too. Beefy. And strong. I'm not really. I wish I were. I'm fifteen but I'm skinny. Slight. Grand says I take after her side of the family—Mother's side—and I'll fill out later. Then the girls will buzz around me like flies. I doubt it. Sometimes I feel that I'll always be waiting in this apartment while my father's out somewhere looking for a part for someone's air conditioner, just the way I am now, with the last Saturday in August slipping away, waiting to show a new tenant his apartment. Tomorrow will be exactly the same, I'll just be waiting for something different, not something better, and— There's the buzzer. The new tenant. The man in 4-C.

Saturday, September 4th

What a busy day—*and* I earned $70! God, I love the feel of new money. I can hardly believe it. I never got this much money at one time before. But the new tenant said I earned it—five hours at $10 an hour, plus $10 for showing him the apartment last Saturday when he came to take exact measurements, plus a $10 tip for being so courteous and helpful. All I really did was say "yes, sir" instead of "yeah" and make a lot of trips to the deli for coffee and snacks. And it wasn't even hard work: I had to stand by the van and watch to make sure nothing got stolen while the moving men were inside carrying stuff. After all, you can't be too careful, even in a fancy neighborhood. And later, he even asked me my opinion, if I thought things looked good where he'd had the movers put them. Once I said no, and he actually moved this expensive-looking chair just because I said so! He kept telling me where the furniture was from—mostly Germany and Austria. I didn't know what he was talking about half the time, but it all sounded very impressive. He said he'd lend me a book about antique furniture once he got his books unpacked. He said he could tell I had exquisite taste naturally, just by the way I admired certain pieces more than others. Maybe he's right. I've always thought I had good taste, I just never had the chance to show it before.

I mean, look at this apartment—everything in it is ugly. Everything except the photograph of Mother taken right before the wedding. And even that's in an ugly frame. The new tenant even asked me all about my family—he'd never met my father, since he'd rented the apartment from the sales agent. I told him about the photograph of Mother. He said he'd like to see it sometime, and I think he meant it. Maybe I'll take it out of that ugly frame before I show it to him. He said I could bring it up tomorrow. Yes! He hired me to help him all day tomorrow. I figure that means around eight hours. And that means $80! God—$150 in two days! If this would only keep up, I could afford that computer I just found out I'll need for school this year. All of the other kids already have PCs at home. Except me. And Juan. I don't have the money. And none of the other tenants ever give me anything except maybe a quarter when I carry a package. And once a dollar when I waited *two* hours for a UPS delivery. They seem to think that just because they tip my father fifty bucks at Christmas, then that includes me. As if my father ever gives me anything except a punch every now and then.

No grown-up ever does anything for me, except Grand. She bakes treats when she can afford the ingredients. She says she wants me to know what Poland tastes like. And she listens to me, not that she really understands what I'm talking about. After all, she's in her seventies. She still believes all these old folk tales she heard back when she was a girl. I don't think she even knows what a computer is. But the new tenant does—I saw this really amazing machine with a printer and stuff being assembled in the extra room. He saw me looking at it and said it was some kind of really new, really advanced model. I certainly have never seen anything quite like it. I wonder why he has such a fancy machine—maybe he uses it for work. I wonder what he does. He never said.

Sunday, September 5th

I only earned $40 today and it's all Grand's fault. When I told Mr. Belliel I could help him from ten to six, I'd forgotten today was Sunday. That's when I walk to Grand's apartment, walk her to her church and sit with her, and then walk her back to her apartment and have a bite of lunch. I could skip the lunch, but I can't skip walking Grand. She's pretty old, and her church is in sort of a bad neighborhood. I'm always asking her why doesn't she go to a church nearer her apartment, but Grand says her church is one of the few where they conduct services in Polish. I can understand that, I guess, but the church is no great shakes—it's just a converted storefront that they got some church bigwig to come bless so it counts as a church. You'd hardly know it's a church, especially from the outside, especially if you couldn't read Polish. And the back entrance in the alley behind looks like it goes into a store, not a church. But it makes Grand happy. I guess hearing the priest speak in Polish reminds her of her girlhood—not that I'm ever very impressed by any of Father Kowalski's sermons. Anyway, after church I tried to eat the lunch Grand had made me as quickly as possible and hoped Grand wouldn't notice I was rushing—but she's pretty observant.

"Someone's in big hurry," she said as I wolfed down my pierogis. "Maybe someone has date?" she added, teasing me.

"No," I told her, "it's the tenant in 4-C, Mr. Belliel. I'm helping him do stuff in his apartment."

"What kind of stuff?"

"Moving and unpacking," I explained. "He's paying me."

"Paying you money?" asked Grand, as if there were another way to be paid.

"Ten dollars an hour," I replied proudly. "But don't tell my father. I'm saving up for a computer."

"Always with these computers," said Grand, taking a sip of this coffee she makes that's so strong it almost jumps up out of the cup all by itself. It's so strong she gives me less than half a cup. She says when I'm older I'll get a full cup. What does she think I am, some kind of kid still? "Hmm," continued Grand, putting down her cup, "ten dollars is good money."

"Ten dollars an hour," I reminded her.

"Very good money," she said, nodding her white-haired head. "Go," she went on. "Today I can do washing up while you earn big dollars."

I kissed her and left. I felt kind of guilty, I'm not sure why. I mean, why shouldn't I earn money for a change? Why should Grand hold me back? Why can't grown-ups help kids instead of hindering them? But I still decided I'd take some of the money I earned and buy Grand something—flowers are always nice.

Mr. Belliel didn't look too happy when I showed up late. Even my good excuse about having to take my grandmother to church didn't seem to impress him. He just raised an eyebrow and said nothing.

"I'm sorry," I said. "If you need me next Sunday, I'll come at ten o'clock and skip church."

Today I helped him hang up all these photographs. They were all small, maybe three by four inches, and put in identical frames of red metal. They were all of people's faces. At first I thought they must be pictures of all the people in his family, and he must have come from a big family, too. Then

I noticed that they were all different races—Caucasian, African-American, Hispanic, Asian, Native American, Arab. I know people can have relatives from all different backgrounds, but usually you don't see so many different races in one family. It was like the United Nations. Also, none of the people looked at all like Mr. Belliel. Mr. Belliel is thin and elegant, with very pale skin. His hair is black and comes to a little point in the middle of his forehead. He combs it straight back. His eyes are sort of green—they're the kind of eyes that seem to look right through you. I'd hate to be in a staring contest with Mr. Belliel! I think he must be around forty years old, but it's hard to tell. My father's forty-three and he looks ten times older than Mr. Belliel. But my father's kind of heavy and always dressed in oily old clothes, and Mr. Belliel always seems to be wearing a suit. Anyway, none of these people looked at all like Mr. Belliel, but I was kind of scared to ask who they were. I didn't want Mr. Belliel to think I was nosy. Or ignorant. I mean, some of the people in the photographs looked familiar. What if they were really famous and I asked who they were?

"These are photographs of various people I've, ah, worked with," explained Mr. Belliel as we hung the pictures up in the long hallway leading from the front of his apartment to the back where the bedroom is. "They are not my family," he added, just as though he'd read my mind, "although sometimes it feels as though they were. Especially now."

I nodded. I wasn't sure what the "especially now" meant, but I didn't want to ask. I wanted Mr. Belliel to think I was as cultured and elegant as he was, not some skinny Polish kid whose father was only a super and whose grandmother cleaned offices a few nights a week.

When I left, Mr. Belliel gave me the $40 in crisp new bills. Just when I was thinking again how nice the new bills felt, Mr. Belliel said, "I love the feel of new money, don't you?"

It's like we really understand each other.

"It's a pity I already gave away my previous computer when I upgraded," said Mr. Belliel out of the blue. "My new model is something of a prototype—it's not on the market yet. Well, when I upgrade next, I'll know what to do with my current model. I've always felt that adults should help younger people, not hinder them. Don't you?"

That did sound good. It's what I've always thought, but I never heard anyone else say it. I shook Mr. Belliel's hand excitedly. He has a firm handshake, and very strong hands. It was nice to have a grown-up besides Grand who is really interested in me. Mr. Belliel said he'd need more help next weekend, so I said I'd reserve both days to help him. I'm sure Grand can get to church alone this one time. I'm so lucky Mr. Belliel moved into 4-C and not some jerk!

Wednesday, September 8th

Now I'm really upset. I can barely write. I can barely even believe it. It's my stupid father. I hate him. I hate him for-

ever. It's going to be all his fault if I can't get that computer
and don't learn how to do stuff on it and don't get into college and have to become a super like him and live in a
basement and wear dirty clothes and get looked down on
by rich snobs.

And it's not just the computer I can't get now. It's
clothes, too. I'd already spent all the money I was going to
earn, at least in my head. I figured I'd put aside 50% of it
to save up for the computer (in case Mr. Belliel doesn't upgrade soon) and spend the rest buying new clothes, like
some new shirts. The one I'm wearing now has been
patched around the elbow at least seventeen times. Grand's
a good sewer, but even she can't make an old shirt look
new. I hate it when the other kids snicker at my clothes. But
I guess I would, too, if I saw me coming.

Now it's no computer, no shirts, no nothing. I knew my
life would never change. I knew my friendship with Mr.
Belliel was too good to be true.

My father says I can't help Mr. Belliel anymore. He got
a good look at him for the first time last night. I guess they
passed in the lobby. He says he doesn't trust him. Just because he's cultured and smart and well-dressed and has
books and stuff in his apartment. He says I shouldn't be
alone with him, that it's not right. I know what he's thinking. He thinks that Mr. Belliel is gay. Maybe he is, but I
don't think so. I don't care, either. My father's kind of big-
oted about a lot of things. He hates gays and blacks and

Puerto Ricans and you name it. Maybe that's why I hate *him.*

He says he's going to go up tomorrow night and tell Mr. Belliel I can't help him anymore. It's so unfair. Everything is unfair. Especially to me.

Thursday, September 9th

There is a God after all! Hooray! I'm saved! Saved!

Tonight, just after our usual dinner out of a can, and right before my father was going to go up and tell Mr. Belliel I couldn't help him anymore, there was a knock on the door.

My father answered it and who should it be but Mr. Belliel, smartly dressed as usual. I could see he made my father really nervous.

"Mr. Mikula," he said politely, extending a white, perfectly manicured hand with a fancy ring on his ring finger that looked sort of like some kind of ruby in a band of gold. My father had no choice but to extend his own rough, filthy hand for Mr. Belliel to shake. I was hoping no dirt would come off on Mr. Belliel. "I'm sorry to disturb you," continued Mr. Belliel politely, smiling over my father's shoulder in my direction, "but I wished to thank you for sparing Vladimir to assist my unpacking."

"Uh, dat's vat I'm vishing to be speaking about," said my

father, stumbling over his words and speaking with an even stronger accent than usual, the way he always does when he has to talk with someone important. He doesn't do too well at other times, either.

"At any rate," went on Mr. Belliel, ignoring my father's words, "I came down to inform Vladimir that my plans have changed. I shall be out of town Friday and Saturday, so I will not require his assistance Saturday as I had foreseen."

"Dat's vat I'm vishing—" tried my father again, when Mr. Belliel interrupted, firmly but politely.

"You see, I am going to be in Philadelphia, visiting with my fiancée."

"Your vat?"

"My fiancée—my future bride. She lives in Philadelphia."

My father's back was to me, but I could imagine how his face looked. Whenever he's relieved, he smiles this goofy smile that shows off his bad teeth.

"Oh," said my father in a different tone than before, "vat a pity. Vlad is looking so much to be helping on dis veek-end."

Mr. Belliel smiled, showing his perfect teeth. "Actually, Vladimir can still assist me," he said. "I shall be back late Saturday night, so I could still use his invaluable help all day Sunday."

"He vill be at apartment as early as you are vishing," said my father, shaking Mr. Belliel's hand for no reason. I thought Mr. Belliel looked a bit grossed out to be shaking my father's hand twice in one evening.

"Nine o'clock would be excellent," said Mr. Belliel, somehow managing to smile as my father kept pumping his hand. "And I shall keep him until, oh, five o'clock, if that's all right."

"Very good, very good," said my father, probably thinking he'd get me to give him some of the money I'd be earning. I was hoping Grand hadn't told him exactly how much it was. I shouldn't have told her.

"I shall see you Sunday, Vladimir," called out Mr. Belliel in his suave voice as he left our apartment.

"So I vas wrong about friend," said my father as the door shut behind Mr. Belliel.

Sunday! I can't wait! And I think I'll bring the photograph of Mother. I want Mr. Belliel to know there's more to my family than just my dumb father.

Sunday, September 12th

Bud *is* right. He really does understand me. He knows I could be somebody—somebody special. Grand says I already am somebody special, but as Bud says, "What does she know? She's from a different world. I doubt she even knows what a computer is. She means well, but that doesn't really help much." That's how I feel, too. I love Grand more than anybody else in this world, but she doesn't really understand me, not the way Bud does.

Like today, for example. I called Grand, to tell her I had to work and couldn't take her to church. I told her with the money I'd be earning I could pay for her to take a taxi, but Grand said no, taxis were made for rich people. And, she added, promises were made for keeping. That made me feel kind of guilty—I *had* given Grand my word I would walk her to and from church every Sunday. But that was before Bud showed up. It's not every day a kid gets the chance to earn $10 an hour! Grand should be happy I'm earning good money, instead of standing in my way. At least, that's what Bud says. He even gave me a present today—this incredibly handsome blue shirt. I've got blue eyes, so I know blue looks pretty good on me. It's as fancy as anything anyone in my school wears—maybe even fancier.

It was right after Bud had given me the shirt. We were sitting on the sofa.

"Perhaps you have something to show me?" inquired Bud.

He was right. I *had* brought Mother's photograph. It was in my knapsack, but I'd felt too embarrassed to bring it out. Now I did.

I handed it to Bud, who examined it carefully. Finally he handed it back to me and said, "No, I've never seen her." At least, that's what I thought he said at the time. He must have said he'd never seen anyone like her. Mother *was* very beautiful: luminous blue eyes, high cheekbones, perfect skin, a glowing smile. I'm glad she lived long enough so I can remember her clearly. Grand always says she was like a flower, and she's right. Not like Grand! She's pretty plain, with her thin white hair just chopped short and no makeup and all her wrinkles and that faded blue dress she always wears. But there's just something about Grand that everybody loves. On warm nights she sits on a folding chair outside her building and everyone on her block stops and says hello, at least on the evenings when she's not cleaning offices.

Anyway, after Bud handed me back the picture we arranged the books in his bedroom. That wasn't hard—he just handed me the books and I put them on the shelf. It's kind of a tall shelf, so I had to climb up and down on this stepladder.

I had the feeling that Bud could have done it all by himself if he'd wanted to. I wasn't sure if he was just feeling kind of lazy or if it was a way he could give me money without it looking like charity. After all, I was there from nine to three and he fed me lunch, too. Then he paid me $60. His wallet was stuffed with money—and I mean stuffed. And he leaves it lying around on the low table near the sofa. It's a good thing I'm so honest. Grand says it runs in her family.

I'd rather good taste ran in our family, the way it seems to in Bud's. Everything in his apartment is beautiful—

whether it's the fabric on his sofa or the silver candlesticks where he puts those elegant long candles. He always keeps a few candles burning, even in the day. He says it adds atmosphere. I think I'm going to take some of the money I'm saving for the computer and clothes and buy some candles and a candlestick. Not that I could afford a silver one, but I'll try to find a nice one. Maybe very gradually I can get my room to look more like Bud's apartment. He'd probably die if he saw those stupid posters I have on my walls. And he'd probably puke if he saw the beige walls, but that was the color paint my father got for free from the landlord. Bud's walls are painted beautiful colors—a little unusual perhaps, but beautiful once you get used to them. Like the living room—it's a dark red. I've never seen a room like it. At first I wasn't so sure I liked it, but now I think it's great, especially how it looks when it's candlelit. I bet it's like some fancy club where Madonna would go.

I like the books, too, in their elegant old bindings. I just wonder what language they're in. I know English and Polish, of course, and I can recognize French, Spanish, and Russian—but Bud's books aren't in any of those languages. But they still look impressive. The only thing I'm not sure I like are those photographs of faces in the hallway, the ones in red frames. It's kind of weird, but when I was at Bud's today, I thought there were a few more than there were last Sunday. But maybe I'm wrong, it's not as if I counted them or anything. But even so, there are a lot. It *is* a long hallway and they run all the way down it. Bud seems very proud of them—I noticed him smiling each time he passed them. He must be a very friendly person.

Tuesday, September 14th

I'm in big trouble. My father gave me seven lashes with his belt. Even Grand will barely speak to me. The thing is, I don't even know how it happened. I don't think it's really my fault.

It all happened last night. Grand came over for one of her weekly visits when she has a night off. That's when she noticed it.

"What on earth has happened to picture of Irina?" she asked, her wrinkled face peering intently at the plastic covering where glass would be in a better frame.

"What do you mean?" I asked. I'd put the picture back when I came down from Bud's on Sunday. I hadn't ripped it or anything. I knew that. I'm always really careful with Mother's photograph.

"Just take look, Vladimir," said Grand in a low voice.

I did, and I couldn't believe my eyes.

"Can you explain?" asked Grand.

I couldn't. I was sure the picture had been all right when I'd brought it back and put it in the frame, but had I really looked at it carefully? I *had* been in kind of a rush to start on my homework. But how could I have missed this? How?

Grand looked back and forth, from me to the picture,

back to me, then back to the picture. Tears were in her blue eyes. Tears were in mine, too. I felt guilty, even though I didn't think it could be my fault.

But there was the picture: it's a large photograph with a white border all around it. At least, the border used to be white. Until now. Now it was sort of singed, like the photograph had been near a fire and the edges had gotten slightly burnt.

But it hadn't been in or even near a fire—it hadn't!

That was when I gulped.

"You are knowing something?" inquired Grand.

"I . . . I took it to show . . . Bud . . ." I began.

"Who is this Bud?"

"Mr. Belliel. The man in 4-C."

"You show picture of Mother to stranger?" demanded Grand, a tear falling down her wrinkled cheek.

"He was interested," I tried to explain. "And I was careful with it. Really."

Grand just shook her head. "Pictures do not jump into fire by self," she said, looking sadly at the photograph.

"It must have been the candle!" I cried suddenly. "Bud—Mr. Belliel—had candles burning! It must have been near one and I didn't see."

"But frame is not burnt."

"I took it out of the frame," I was forced to admit.

"And why that?"

"It's ugly," I said, bowing my head.

Grand shook her head. "Ugly frame does not make photograph ugly. Nothing on earth can be making picture of my Irina ugly. She is beauty."

"But look," I said, taking the picture from Grand, "we can trim the border—the picture's still all right. See?"

Grand just nodded. That was when my father appeared, back from checking the hot water heater. He was even more upset than Grand. That's when he took me in the back and hit me. For once Grand didn't even try to stop him. She must think he doesn't hit me with all his strength. But he does. And he's strong. And I'm skinny. That makes it hurt more.

Now I'm grounded till Friday, stuck again in this dark ugly apartment. I have to come straight home from school. I can't hang around with Juan. His father's a super, too, but he's a lot nicer than mine. And I can't go up and see Bud. But that's okay. He'd notice if I groaned every time I sat down, and I don't want him to know that my father hits me. He might not like me anymore if he knew what kind of family I come from. I mean, it was only a photograph, and it wasn't even really damaged, just the border. It's not like it was taken professionally and framed nicely, the way the portraits are up in Bud's apartment.

Thursday, September 16th

Now they want me to bring the shirt back. My father says it's not right to accept gifts from tenants, even though he takes their bottles of vodka at Christmas. Grand agrees.

Since when does she always take my father's side? And I only got to wear the shirt twice. And it was the only time any of the rich snobs at my school even seemed to notice me. I'll never get such a wonderful shirt again as long as I live. I can't even begin to imagine how much it cost. I'd give anything to keep this shirt, and then to get some pants to go with it. Then I'd be as fancy as Forrest Carrington III and J. D. "Skip" Basingwell, Jr., and all the other rich snobs I go to school with. Even Juan was impressed. When I met him on the way to lunch, he said, "Hey man, wha' happened? Did some rich relative die an' leave you big bucks?"

Now that's all over. What if Bud gets offended when I return the shirt and doesn't want to be my friend anymore? What if he doesn't want me to help him out? What if I never earn enough money to get that really outstanding computer I need? I just learned I'm going to need a computer for my English and history projects.

Just when I start getting somewhere, leave it to my family to step in and stop me—even Grand.

I'll go and see Bud tomorrow. Friday. That'll be the day— the day my new streak of good luck comes to an end and I'm stuck forever being little Vladimir Mikula, total nobody.

Friday, September 17th

"We can work this out, you and I."

That's what he said. There I was, back in the candlelit

room. He even put his hand on my shoulder, man to man. He must be the greatest person I've ever known. When he put his hand on my shoulder, I felt this warm rush go right through my body, like a wave of hot flame.

I'd brought the shirt back up, but before I could open my mouth he began speaking.

"So your family does not like you accepting gifts," Bud said in his low, even voice, a faint smile on his lips but anger in his eyes.

"No," I kind of mumbled. "They . . . well . . ."

"They wish to stand in your way," said Bud, finishing the sentence for me. "You finally meet someone who can help you, someone who cares about the real you—and they do not like it. Sounds suspiciously like jealousy to me."

I hadn't thought of it that way. But I bet Bud's right. They never had a rich friend who wanted to help them. My father works for a lot of rich people, but it's not like they care about him. As long as they get hot water and the halls are clean, they don't even know he's alive. And Grand cleans offices where a lot of fancy people work, but they don't even see her unless they're working really late.

"I have to give the shirt back," I said sadly as Bud got up and left the elegant living room without a word. I heard him next in the kitchen, fiddling around with some glasses.

Soon he reappeared, carrying a silver tray. On it were two glasses—two wineglasses. With wine in them! Red wine.

Bud sat down in the armchair across from me and smiled.

"You appear distraught," he said. "I thought a sip of wine might be called for."

"But I'm only fifteen—" I began.

"That means," interrupted Bud, "that you are a young man ready to make up his own mind."

"But my father and Grand say I can't—"

"Can't do anything fun or sophisticated," Bud broke in, finishing the sentence for me. "I have only put a few swallows in your glass," he explained, picking up his glass and swishing around the wine. "Such a lovely color," he observed, half to himself. "Red. My favorite." For a moment he appeared lost in thought, like he was remembering something really special. Then he began speaking to me again.

He said a lot—so much I'm amazed I can remember it all. But it made so much sense, it was like hearing something I've always known but had never heard put into words before. Bud said that my father and Grand must for some reason be opposed to my happiness. They wanted to saddle me with their small lives. It was almost as if they were in league together—in league to deny me opportunities. Bud thought they must suffer from lack of vision. Or maybe they're scared that if I become rich and successful I'll be too good for them. But he said that was *their* problem—it shouldn't be mine. He said I was a young man, ready for life. Real life. Success and glamour and beautiful possessions—all the things money can buy. But he told me I'd never succeed until I started making my own way—the way forward. Away from my father's temper and Grand's

apron strings. He said I was ready to start being a gentleman. I liked the sound of that. It made me smile. Bud
smiled, too. Then he raised his glass. So did I.

"To Vladimir Mikula, gentleman," he said, and drank.

I drank, too.

The first sip burned like fire, but the second was better.
And the third swallow was best of all. But that was all there
was. Bud wouldn't give me any more.

He said he didn't want me becoming inebriated. And he
said we had much to discuss.

He was talking about the shirt.

"*They* wish you to return it," he said. "*You* long to keep
it. And why not? It is your right. So keep it you shall. You
shall be as fancy as the other students in your school. You
will not be a nobody for long. Trust me."

Then, reaching with his long arms, Bud produced a flat-
tish box from behind his armchair. He handed it to me.

"Open it," Bud almost ordered me.

"They're nicer than any that Forrest or Skip have!" I
cried, admiring this pair of charcoal-gray pants that were so
elegant-looking I couldn't believe they were really for me.

"They are for you," said Bud, smiling. "They go well
with the shirt, do they not?"

"Perfectly!" I cried. "I won't be teased if I wear pants like
this with that shirt! They are so cool!"

"Now Forrest Carrington the Third and 'Skip'
Basingwell will start treating you the way you deserve,"
commented Bud.

"But I can't keep them!" I wailed. "You know my father and Grand don't want me accepting gifts from tenants."

Bud smiled. "We need not say they are gifts," he said.

When I asked what he meant, Bud started explaining.

He told me he'd give me the shirt and pants, but we'd tell my father and Grand that they were payment instead of money for having worked for him. Since they didn't object to my working for Bud, they shouldn't object if we've arranged that Bud pay me with clothing instead of cash. Of course, Bud told me, he'll continue to pay me cash—I'd just tell my father and Grand otherwise. It would be our own little secret.

"But that's lying!" I couldn't help bursting out.

A flicker of impatience flashed across Bud's eyes. Then he explained it so it all made sense. It made so much sense I remember each word.

"It's not really lying," he told me. "Not if it helps you and harms no one. You see, this, ah, friend of mine who owns a clothing store owes me many favors. These articles of clothing are actually overstock which he gives me in payment for past favors. But your father and grandmother could not be expected to understand that. They are hardly sophisticated. Nor could they be expected to understand that I wish to help you—that I see great promise in you. That I know with a bit of guidance, you could be far more than you are now. You could be the person you dream of being. And I like, ah, helping people. It is part of my job, if you will. My work enables me to share a great deal. And my employer, generous soul that he is, likes to know I am sharing. I have even taken the liberty of mentioning you to him. He was most encouraging."

Wow! Even somebody's boss thinks I'm going to be someone special! I smiled. And of course I was interested to know that Bud had a boss. I thought he worked for himself. Maybe when I was older his boss would hire me! I began thinking of Bud and me working together, making and spending lots of money, and his boss saying I was his best new employee and giving me a big raise.

"Actually," said Bud, "my employer is always looking for new talent. That is why I mentioned you to him. He has advanced the careers of many of my, ah, friends."

I smiled again, thanking God for the day Bud moved into the building. Then I began feeling a little guilty about lying.

"But Bud," I said softly, "do I have to lie to Grand and my father?"

Bud fixed me with his gaze. "Look at it this way. Your father hits you. Your grandmother doesn't stop it. That is more wrong than anything you are doing."

"How did you know he—" I began. I hadn't told. I'd promised myself I never would.

Bud just gave a faint smile. "Let us say the walls have ears," he said, making me wonder if the sound had traveled up the light shaft. I didn't see how it would. "At any rate," continued Bud, "you are actually doing your father and grandmother a favor. I know you, Vlad. When you succeed in life, you will be generous with them. But if you do not succeed, then how will you be able to assist them? And looking good is the beginning of doing well. Trust me."

So after arranging to help him all day the following Sunday, it was time to go. Bud was expecting some important business messages. I don't know if they were coming over his fax machine or on his computer. I left clutching my new shirt and pants, wishing I had even more clothes so I could impress the other kids more than one day in a row.

Saturday, September 18th—morning

Boy am I embarrassed. I just have to get it out and into my diary before I die of embarrassment.

I ran into Bud in the front hall when I was on my way to the hardware store for my father. He was with this beautiful woman. It looked like they were going out to lunch in some fancy restaurant. They were both dressed up. He was wearing this perfectly tailored black suit and the woman was wearing this tight bright red dress and red high heels. She had bright red lipstick that accented the paleness of her face. Her hair was red, too, and pulled back in a tight braid. She looked like a movie star. She also looked a little like Bud, like his sister. But that wasn't the embarrassing part— thank God I didn't ask if she was his sister! Phew!

"Vladimir," said Bud, "I would like to introduce my fiancée, Bella."

Bella gave me the most glorious smile. It made me feel like I was the most interesting person she'd ever met.

Then she gave me a kiss on either cheek. It was so exciting, both cheeks felt like they were on fire. I'm sure I was blushing.

"What a pleasure it is to meet you, Vladimir," she said in a sexy, husky voice. Then she turned and said, "Darling, why did you not tell me how handsome Vladimir is? And so young, too, so very young."

I blushed even more.

Bella smiled back at me and then turned and said, "You have done well, Bub, to find such a one!"

"See you tomorrow, Vlad," Bud—I mean *Bub!*—called out as he and Bella made their way to the front door.

I've been calling him the wrong name for days! Last Sunday, he asked me to stop calling him Mr. Belliel and call him by his first name. I was sure he said Bud, which I figured was a nickname. But I must have misheard. His name is *Bub*—at least, that's what Bella called him. Now I don't know what to call him—Bud or Bub. Maybe Bub is just a special name his girlfriend calls him. Or maybe it's what everyone calls him. I wish I knew. He'd think I was a real jerk if I asked. Maybe I'll be able to see something in his apartment with his name written on it. Then I can know for sure without looking like a jerk.

But at least, my father bought the story about being paid in clothes instead of money. All I have to do now is sneak the money into my bank account. It's a good thing I already have one—not that it's ever had more than around $24 in it! But that shouldn't be too hard. And I have to convince Grand. Sometimes she's smarter than my father. But I can do it. Bud—or Bub?—says it's good practice, that all great businessmen have to lie sometimes if they want to succeed. And I want to succeed. As Bud says, I *deserve* to succeed.

Saturday, September 18th—afternoon

It's not been a great day. I'd forgotten I promised Grand I'd take her to church tomorrow to make up for skipping last week and leaving lunch early the week before. But now I can't—I promised Bub I'd help him out. Let's face it: I'm not a kid anymore, I'm a young man. Bub says I am, and he knows more than Grand or my father. He's been around. So if I want to work on Sunday instead of taking Grand to that dumb little church she goes to that doesn't even look like a church, that should be my decision.

But not according to Grand.

We were talking on the phone. I'd gotten her to believe Bub was paying me in clothes now, when the question of Sunday came up. I could almost see the hurt look on her face when I told her I couldn't take her. I know I'm all she has left—Mother was Grand's only child, and I'm Mother's only child. But that's not my fault. Just because I'm her only grandchild shouldn't mean I have to give up my life to take her places when I could be earning money. Besides, it's like Bub says—if I do well, then I'll help Grand out with some of the money I earn. That's more important than taking her to church. Someday she'll be really old and need me to support her. If I'm doing well I'll be able to. And in the meantime I'll buy her flowers. I meant to the other week, but I never got around to it. After all, I was grounded for a few days. They shouldn't have grounded me if they expect me to go buy flowers.

Sunday, September 19th

Seven hours at $10 per hour = $70.00! That makes $250.00 total. I never had so much money in my life! I never had *any* money in my life. And Bub gave me another shirt and a pair of pants. He says I should be able to impress the other kids for more than one day in a row. He says it will be easy sneaking money into the bank. Grand and my father will never know. They really believe Bub is paying me in clothes, not cash. What pushovers!

And his name *is* Bub. I checked—he'd left a note from Bella out on the coffee table. It's kind of a weird name, but I like it. It sounds kind of dumb at first, like when someone on the street says, "Hey, bub!" But once you've seen the real Bub, the name starts sounding as elegant as he is.

"It is easy for a young person from a limited background to make mistakes," said Bub out of nowhere. He didn't say what he was talking about, but I guessed it was me calling him the wrong name. "That is why such a young person needs guidance. He may feel sure he knows something, but he can be wrong."

Anyway, today I helped Bub put his files in alphabetical order. It seems the movers had dropped them when Bub left his last apartment. Hmm, I wonder where that was. So, he and I got busy and started alphabetizing.

It took a long time, there were so many of them. Each file had someone's name printed on the top. Inside the files were mostly computer printouts. I couldn't help but glance at a few. They contained a little biographical information, then a whole lot of information about their jobs and how much they earned and awards and stuff they had won, and whether they'd bought cars and houses or got married or had children. It seemed like everybody in the files was really successful, just the way Bub is. I was wondering about this, when Bub must have noticed me looking thoughtful.

"They *are* all highly successful people," he said as I handed him all the files beginning with the letter L. "They did not use to be, but then when we started working together, well, let us say everything changed. You may look at the files," he continued. "They might be of interest."

So I looked more carefully. There were lists of goals for each person, then the date they began working with Bub (or the company Bub works for, I wasn't sure). Then there were dates when each of their goals was met. It was amazing—all their dreams came true. Each file also contained a contract, written in fancy calligraphy, between the person in the file and Bub. I checked his name on the contract. In big bold letters he'd written "B. Bub Belliel." Kind of an impressive name. I wondered what the "B" stood for. Then at the bottom there was a big seal put on with wax, just like on an old-fashioned document in a museum. I wished *my* name was on a document, and *my* list of dreams was there, too. Let's see: a nicer apartment, that new computer, a new wardrobe, a scholarship to a good college, a girlfriend. I wondered if Bub could arrange all that. He must know a lot of people or something. I'd always heard about people like that—people who know all the right people and can arrange anything. Wow—to think I'd actually met one and he liked me! I did kind of wonder what the contract actually said—I couldn't read it. I think it was in the same language as the books were that I helped Bub shelve.

At that moment a fax came in and Bub went to read it. He came back smiling and handed it to me. It concerned someone named Walter Schaffer. It was confirming the fact that he'd been made a vice president of the advertising agency where he worked and had gotten an enormous raise. And I mean enormous. If I earned just the amount of his increase, I'd think I was rich. If I earned his entire salary I think I'd die of shock!

Bub had me put it in Walter's file. I noticed one of his goals had been a promotion and a big raise. I started wondering if Bub or his boss had helped Walter get his promotion and raise. I mean, how could they do that, unless Walter worked for the corporation that Bub's boss was president of?

It kind of made me wonder exactly what Bub did for a living.

"Perhaps this makes you curious as to my precise profession," said Bub as I handed him the "M"s and the "N"s.

I nodded, trying to look nonchalant.

"For now," Bub went on, "we can say that I am a sort of trader. It is a bit more complicated than that, but it gets the idea across."

I nodded again, even though I was still confused. I guess Bub must work on Wall Street, trading stocks and stuff to help people make money so they can make their dreams come true. I wasn't quite sure how that would help someone get a promotion, but maybe Bub said he'd invest in Walter's agency if they gave Walter a promotion. That would be sort of a trade, I guess. Or maybe once you started working with Bub, your luck changed. Grand says some people are naturally lucky, just the way some people are naturally good or bad. Bub must be both good *and* lucky, and now some of his luck just has to rub off on me.

I think it already has—I've got $250 and two new shirts and pairs of pants to prove it!

I was so happy tonight when I came home and hid my money and tried on my new clothing that I barely thought about how bad Grand must feel not to have me take her to church two Sundays in a row.

Wednesday, September 22nd

I finally stopped by Grand's with some flowers. I bought daisies. They only cost $3.25 because they weren't too big a bunch. If I spend all my money on flowers I'll never save enough for that computer.

Grand was really excited, and not about the flowers (although she liked them, too). No, she sat me down at her kitchen table.

"Vladski," she said, using her old nickname for me, "for you I have big news."

"Yes?" I said, wondering what kind of big news Grand could come up with.

"For you I am finding good job," she announced proudly.

"But I'm only fifteen," I reminded her. "You know I can't work legally."

"It is for friend," she explained, "so payment is under table."

"But Bub—Mr. Belliel—is already employing me."

"He is stranger. I find work with friend. And not just friend. Priest."

"Yeah?" I said, waiting for details.

"Reverend Father Kowalski is needing boy to be helping

his brother who is owning store next to church. To sweep and help customers. Two afternoons a week and on Saturday."

"But that's when I work for Bub sometimes!" I argued. "He's counting on me!"

"So is brother of Father Kowalski."

"How much does he pay?" I wanted to know.

"Because is under table, and no tax, he is paying you three dollars the hour."

"Three dollars an hour!" I burst out. "Bub pays me ten—"

"I am thinking that neighbor is paying you in clothing, not money," interrupted Grand, looking at me sharply.

"He does. I meant, um, that the clothes are, well, they're worth ten dollars an hour."

"I see," said Grand. "Now you can be earning money from brother of Father Kowalski and clothing from neighbor."

"Not if I'm working for this Kowalski guy when Bub needs me," I pointed out. "And he needs me on weekends most of all."

"I know," said Grand glumly. I guess she's still mad at me for missing the last two Sundays, despite the flowers. "I have idea," she said suddenly. "Maybe brother of Father Kowalski will hire you three afternoons in week and you can be free on Saturday to get fancy clothes. Then on Sunday you are free to escort Grandmother."

I nodded. I didn't like the idea, but what could I do? I hated hurting Grand's feelings.

Maybe it wouldn't work out. Maybe this Kowalski guy would find somebody else. Maybe Bub would have a better idea.

Maybe Grand would just butt out of my life.

Thursday, September 23rd

Good news and bad news.

At least, I think it's good news.

I'm just back from dropping in at Bub's. He's always so glad to see me it makes me happy. I love just going into his candlelit room. He even stopped working at his computer to chat with me, listening intently while I told him about the job Grand had found for me.

"I see no problem here," he said.

My jaw must have dropped, because Bub smiled broadly.

"No," he continued, "I think it will come in most—ah, useful."

"Useful?"

"Quite so. If you are earning money at Mr. Kowalski's establishment—and I wonder what manner of store it is— that gives you an excuse to be putting money into your savings account, does it not? And of course, into that account will go not only whatever paltry sum Mr. Kowalski will pay you, but the far more generous amount I give you. Otherwise, even your father might ask himself why you are conducting business at the bank. You needn't work there long—we can figure a way out of it at a later date. But in the short run it should come in tremendously useful."

"You're right," I agreed. "It's not like my father or Grand will check how much money I have in my account. It's not like either of them knows anything about finance, anyway."

"Quite right," said Bub, smiling. "Both your father and grandmother are hopelessly naive about such things. It is a wonder you are such a sophisticated young man."

I bowed my head modestly.

"There *is* one problem," continued Bub a moment later. "And that is when you will work for me."

"I thought Saturday would—" I began, but Bub interrupted sharply.

"Saturdays are out," he said flatly. "I need you Sundays from now on, and Sundays only. All day, too."

"But that's when I take—" I started, and once again Bub interrupted.

"I know all that," he said. "The choice is yours."

I didn't have to think more than five seconds before deciding. Anybody would have decided the same thing. I'm a young man on my way up, not an escort service.

"Good," said Bub when I'd told him my decision. "I shall see you Sunday morning at nine o'clock sharp."

"Yes, sir," I said. "Nine o'clock sharp."

I left feeling proud of myself. It was a grown-up decision and I decided it quickly and in a grown-up way. I know Bub thought I'd done the right thing—I could tell by his pleased expression. That counts for a lot.

Grand was less pleased, but that's her problem. She tried to argue but I told her I had to go, that I had lots of home-work to get done and couldn't spend the entire night talk-ing on the phone. Then I hung up. I didn't actually hang up on her, but I didn't hang around arguing. After all, I am a young man on the way up.

But I did feel kind of bad afterwards. To feel better I looked through this fashion magazine Bub had put on top of the recycling bin. You're supposed to put things inside, but he'd left it on top. Maybe he doesn't like getting his hands dirty—the inside of the bin can be kind of gross. It's not like my father ever cleans it carefully. He's got no aes-thetic sense, not like I do.

Anyway, the stuff in the magazine was outstanding. I wouldn't mind having one of each. The handsomest thing was this pair of wool pants in this unusual blue-gray color. I wish I could wear something like that, but—

Oh damn, my father's home and he wants me to heat up soup for dinner. What does he think I am, some kind of slave?

Friday, September 24th

Working for Joe Kowalski in his scummy locksmith shop isn't like working for Bub. And it's not just the money, though that's really pathetic. It's slave labor to work for $3 an hour! If he hired a sixteen-year-old, Kowalski would have to cough up minimum wage. And he acts like he's doing me this big favor. And his fat priest brother comes waddling in from next door to make sure I'm not goofing off. He says I should make my grandmother proud of me. He should make *his* grandmother proud of *him* and go tell his brother to give me a raise. I live in fear that one of my classmates will come in and see me all sweaty behind the counter, learning how to pound out keys. That's the only good thing about it—it's far away in a bad neighborhood, so it's not likely that any of my snooty classmates would even set foot there in a million years. Only Juan might, but then he wouldn't care anyway.

And when there's a pause in business, instead of letting me relax for a few minutes the way Bub would, I have to go next door to Father Kowalski's church and do odd jobs like sweeping and straightening up the pews.

"Now this would make your grandmother proud," Father Kowalski intones, patting his fat stomach as I puff away, pushing the heavy pews around all by myself. You'd think at least he'd help me. Even when I'm working for Bub *he* always lends a hand, and *he's* a gentleman.

And he's even too lazy to go open the door for me—Father Kowalski, I mean. I have to take Joe's set of keys, go out the back door of Kowalski's Locksmith Shop into the alley, then go in the back door of the church. That way I can let myself in without Father Kowalski even having to walk fifteen feet to open the door. I hate that alley, it's so spooky and deserted, even in the day. And it seems like I've been there a million times because that's how I go in with Grand when she gets to church early and does some straightening up for Father Kowalski. I guess he doesn't like her coming in the front door, because then other parishioners might see and know he was there, and come in to talk with him. Then he'd have to do some work. He's so lazy I'm surprised he even bothers giving the sermon himself. The only thing he's not lazy about is giving me grief for not being in church the last few Sundays. There I was, doing favors and getting grief at the same time. Bub would say these people are really unsophisticated, and they are. I wonder what he meant when he said he'd figure a way out of this job at a later date. How later? I've only worked there one day and I'm already sick of it. I'm too good for this kind of slave labor, I know I am. Much too good.

Sunday, September 26th

"You *are* too good for them," said Bub. "I am glad you can see that now."

It was after we'd finished working, and the work hadn't been too hard, either—just some more filing and hanging up a few more pictures in the hallway. Next time I'm going to count them. It feels like every time I'm up at Bub's, there are more than the time before. I wonder where they all come from.

"They shouldn't treat you that way," continued Bub as he

and I sipped on our coffee and nibbled some delicious cookies. "You are better than they are. It's just a matter of time before you find your wings and take flight. Yes—take flight. And I can make it happen."

I swallowed my coffee and nodded knowingly. But I didn't quite know what Bub was really talking about. How could he make things happen? I'm only fifteen. What was he going to make happen?

"Here," he said unexpectedly, reaching behind the sofa and pulling out a box. "You have had a hard day, working for that slave driver Kowalski. And his nasty brother," added Bub, shuddering at the mention of Father Kowalski. He seems to dislike him even more than Joe.

"What is it?" I asked hopefully, eyeing the box.

"I thought you might like it," said Bub, a light shining in his green eyes.

Forgetting to act suave and nonchalant, I tore the box open. My jaw dropped. I didn't know what to say.

"This color and style suits you to a T," commented Bub, looking pleased with himself. "Blue-gray accents your coloring—your black hair and blue eyes. A gentleman always knows how best to attire himself."

There they were—the pants I'd admired in the magazine, the wool ones, the blue-gray ones.

"I believe the size is correct," continued Bub. "But you can pop up later and let me know."

"I—I—" I started, but Bub interrupted.

"No need to be embarrassed. You deserve nice things,

beautiful, expensive things. I am able to provide them. But soon we shall arrange for you to provide for yourself. I feel you are ready. So does my employer. Speaking of which, I am expecting him to contact me shortly. We shall be discussing you. He is most interested in you, Vlad."

So I left, clutching my new pants. Proud to be the topic of discussion between Bub and his boss. But worried, too. About offending Bub. It's the pants. Bub doesn't know it, but I'm totally allergic to wool. I break out in a rash. I can't wear wool anything. It runs in the family on Mother's side. I wish I could wear stylish woolen stuff, but I can't. I just can't. What do I do now? What if Bub can't return them? I felt guilty before, accepting money when I hadn't really worked that hard, and now Bub has got me these pants I'll never be able to wear.

I have to solve this problem. I'll try to do what's sophisticated. And grown-up. I just don't know what that would be. I'd ask Grand, but she's probably still mad at me for not taking her to church today.

Well, who needs her anyway.

Monday, September 27th

Grand called last night. I think she was trying to make me feel guilty about not taking her to church. Bub said she'd try something like that. And she was pretty clever about it—she kept not bringing it up. She was probably trying to make *me* bring it up and apologize and all that, but no way. There's no reason I should apologize for growing up and starting to make my way in the world. Bud said Grand and my father would try to hold me back. Some people are scared of change. I'm not one of them. Anyway, to talk about something with Grand, I mentioned Bub had given me wool pants that I never would be able to wear and I didn't know what to do about it.

"Is not good to be offending important man," said Grand. "Rich man, too. You must be telling him pants are best you have ever seen and you are saving them for important occasion like dinner with priest."

I knew she'd get the priest in there somehow!

Now I don't know what to do. Bub *is* a rich, important man, and what happens if I offend him? Would he tell his boss not to hire me? Would I stay stuck here in my dumb life for ever and ever?

Tuesday, September 28th

He *is* a gentleman, not at all like my father. And sophisticated, not like Grand.

I dropped by Bub's. I'd decided to take Grand's advice, and tell him the pants fit really well and I was saving them for an important occasion. I wasn't going to say dinner with Father Kowalski—I've noticed Bub cringe every time I mention Father Kowalski.

Anyway, before I could open my mouth, Bub started speaking in his crisp, elegant voice.

"Vlad," he said, laying a hand on my shoulder, "can you imagine my embarrassment? I had totally forgotten you had mentioned the fact that you were allergic to wool."

"I did?" I said. I'd totally forgotten it, too.

"It was a while back. However, I should have recalled it—one should always recall little details about one's friends. How foolish I was to then give you wool pants! You must bring them back and I'll exchange them for ones more suitable. In fact, you could come with me and select the pair you most prefer. And perhaps a shirt or two as well. How about tomorrow?"

"I work tomorrow," I said sadly. "Wednesday, Friday, and Saturday."

"You could call in sick," suggested Bub, then shook his head. "No, the time is not yet right. We shall go Thursday. Meet me as soon as you return from school."

"Sounds good!" I said, all relieved. "Boy," I confessed, "I was nervous about offending you by not liking the pants. I was going to tell you they were great."

Bub looked hard at me.

"I cannot imagine who gave you such inane advice," he remarked. "If someone does something unacceptable, they should be told immediately. It might appear harsh, but in truth you are doing them a favor. This is how business operates. This is how people can improve their performance. My employer, thoughtful soul that he is, feels this strongly.

He would be gravely disappointed to hear you had lied to me. I am grateful this did not occur."

"It was all Grand's idea," I informed Bub.

"It sounds like a prime example of her unsophisticated style of thought," replied Bub. "I am glad you have outgrown such littleness."

Wednesday, September 29th

"Is not good manners to be insulting people," stated Grand in a firm voice after I'd repeated some of Bub's observations. "Am I right, Father?"

"Absolutely," said Father Kowalski, patting his stomach. "The Christian response is to be always grateful and thankful. As ye give so shall ye receive."

"But Bub says—"

"Tell us later, Vladimir," broke in Joe Kowalski. "The floor needs sweeping."

So I swept while Grand and the Kowalskis chatted. Grand had stopped in the shop after doing a favor for Father Kowalski at the church: she was embroidering some seat covers—for Father Kowalski's fat rear end, I couldn't help but think. She wanted to thank Joe Kowalski for hiring me. And she probably was trying to make me feel guilty again for not taking her to church. Bub said I should never feel guilty for doing what's right for me.

"About trousers," called Grand as I swept out the back of the shop, "did you tell neighbor they are handsome?"

"No, Grand. I told him the truth. It's like I was saying before, if someone does something unacceptable, they should be told immediately. You're really doing them a favor."

"Sounds like strange favor to old lady," commented Grand. At first I couldn't understand what she was saying because of this loud jingling noise. It turned out Grand was adding the keys to the back door of the church to her key ring. Probably Father Kowalski wanted her to come back every day and do more embroidering. And with her own set of keys, Father Kowalski wouldn't even have to get up to let her in! Those Kowalski brothers must be the laziest people in town!

"No way," I countered, once I'd understood Grand over the sound of the keys. "Bub was glad I'd told him. In fact, he was so glad he's taking me shopping tomorrow to replace the pants and maybe pick up a shirt or two."

"Who's this Bub person?" asked Father Kowalski.

"Neighbor of grandson," explained Grand. "Vlad is working for him and receiving payment in clothing."

"Sounds fishy to me—a grown man buying a boy clothes," commented Joe. "What is he, a fashion designer?"

"No," I burst out, not liking Joe's tone, "he's . . . he's a trader. Very successful, too."

"What does he trade, fashion hints?" mocked Joe, laughing at his own dumb joke.

"No," I said, "he trades . . . he trades . . . He just trades."

When Joe Kowalski had finished guffawing, and after a quick glance to make sure I was sweeping carefully, he said, "It still sounds weird to me. There are a lot of strange types in New York City, and he could be one of them."

"Son-in-law has met this Bub and is saying is all right," pronounced Grand.

Joe Kowalski snorted. "From what I've heard of Tomasz Mikula, your son-in-law is not exactly a brain surgeon."

"No," replied Grand, "son-in-law is super." Then she got what Joe was saying. "No," she said more softly, "Irina never say Tomasz has strong mind." Grand always claimed my father was handsome when he was young, but I kind of doubt it.

"If I were you," said Father Kowalski as he stood up and prepared to leave, "I'd arrange to meet this neighbor before I allowed an impressionable youngster like Vladimir to spend more time with him. I don't care how rich he is."

"Leave Bub alone!" I cried from the back of the shop, hitting the broom handle against the wall for emphasis. "And I'm not a youngster, either," I added, which made all the grown-ups laugh at me, even Grand.

Thursday, September 30th

Two pairs of pants and *three* shirts! Now I have almost a week's worth of clothes to impress the kids in my school!

And Bub says the best is yet to come. I wonder what he means.

Bub's friend runs this fancy men's clothing store on Madison Avenue. Actually, I don't think Mr. Harrison is a friend—he's more like a business partner or something. He seemed kind of nervous around Bub. Maybe he owes him money. He was nervous around me, too, like he kept wanting to say something but couldn't find the right moment or the right words. Maybe he just didn't like the clothes I was picking out. It was weird, too—he looked so familiar, but I couldn't quite place him. But I would bet I'd seen his face somewhere before.

I never saw so much beautiful clothing in my life. And the prices! Grand would have a fit! *She* does all her shopping at the Salvation Army. And I don't think my father *ever* goes shopping. He must find his wardrobe lying on the side-walk. There sure must be a lot of rich people in New York—the store was jammed with people, and they were all buying clothes by the ton. This one guy spent more than $2,000 in less than half an hour. I know, because I heard Mr. Harrison call in the information to the credit card company.

Mr. Harrison must be making money hand over fist. And he's pretty lucky, too. I know this because while Bub was chatting with Mr. Harrison, I overheard these two guys next to me talking. According to them, Mr. Harrison's store was about to go out of business—they'd even put "Going Out of Business" signs in the window—when all of a sudden they had a big turnaround. And ever since then it had become one of the most successful shops in the city. He'd even opened branches in Boston and Philadelphia.

Mr. Harrison served me when I was making my selections. Bub just watched—he said I should get used to selecting good clothing. "You need to develop both your taste and your bearing," he told me.

Mr. Harrison was a short, middle-aged man with a sad expression. I wouldn't be so sad if I were making that much money. Maybe he was just having a bad day.

Anyway, I finally selected a pair of jet-black cotton pants that look really wicked and Bub let me get this gorgeous pair of light brown suede pants. They're the fanciest thing I've ever seen. I'd read about suede pants in articles on rock stars, but I never thought I'd have a pair, never! And I also picked out a silk shirt. I was scared to look at the price tag, but Bub called out that money was no object.

The only bad part was when I thought that even if I do impress the kids in my school and they start liking me, I still couldn't bring them to my apartment. It's too gross. Maybe Bub would let me take them to *his,* and I could pretend it was mine.

Mr. Harrison put it all into bags, carefully wrapped in tissue paper so nothing would get wrinkled. I noticed Bub didn't pay him—I guess Mr. Harrison must really owe Bub a lot of money. When he was done with the wrapping, Mr. Harrison handed me the bag. He looked even sadder than before, kind of worried, too. He took a deep breath and seemed nervous, like he was about to take a dive off a really high diving board.

"Young man," he said in a low voice as if he were afraid of being overheard, eyeing Bub, who was almost going out the door, "listen to me. I advise you to take care—"

"Yes," called out Bub in a cheerful voice from the door, "good idea, Mr. Harrison. Be sure to let Vladimir know the proper way to take care of his new clothing."

Mr. Harrison looked more nervous. "Yes, Mr. Belliel, that's just what I was about to do."

"Such a disappointing little man," said Bub as we climbed into a taxi a few minutes later.

"What do you mean?" I wanted to know.

"For years he prays for success, and now that he's finally attained it, all he does is worry. I doubt he even enjoys his newfound riches. What a waste."

"That's for sure," I agreed, thinking Mr. Harrison must be a major fool. "I'd give anything to be so rich and success-ful!"

"That is just what I'm counting on," said Bub, patting me warmly on the shoulder.

Friday, October 1st

I could kill Grand. Why does she have to butt her wrinkled old face into my business, anyway? It's all that stupid Father

Kowalski's fault. Him and his bushy-eyebrowed slave driver of a brother.

I got home from Kowalski's Locksmith Shop around seven o'clock with all of $12 in my pocket. They don't even pay my subway fare and that's not cheap. Anyway, I let myself in and there were Grand and my father, sitting at the table. I knew they were having a serious discussion, because the second I entered they both shut up and looked nervous. Especially Grand.

"Sit down, Vladimir," said Grand in a husky voice, like she was choking back some big emotion. "I am following today advice of Mr. Kowalski and am meeting neighbor, your Mr. Bellal—"

"Belliel," I corrected.

"I am meeting neighbor," continued Grand, ignoring me, "and . . . and . . . well, I am deciding he is not . . . not good man."

"But he is! He's the best! Just look what he's done for me! More than you've ever done!"

Grand looked hurt but she kept on talking.

"I am seeing this kind of, um, person before, in Poland when young. He is not good man. He is bad. Very bad. You are forbidden to seeing him again. Your father is agreeing."

My father nodded his stupid head. "Forbidden," he repeated like a parrot.

"But why?" I screamed. "I don't know what dumb things my father told you, but—"

"Your father is telling me nothing. I am seeing with own eyes. Neighbor is bad. I am not wishing to discuss more about it. Decision is final."

"Final," repeated my idiot parrot of a father.

"No!" I hollered. "Bub's my best friend! You can't stop me from seeing him, no matter what you do!"

"You may not see him," stated my father, slamming his big fist down on the table.

"I'll do what I want to do! You're just jealous because I'm moving up in the world and you're not! You're both pathetic jerks!"

My father was raising his fist to hit me when Grand, who seemed to be crying a little bit, interceded.

"Go to room, Vlad," she said. "Now."

So I did. I'm so angry all I can do is write in this diary. It's a good thing my brainless father can't read it. Then he'd know I'm still going to see Bub even if it means sneaking up the fire escape or running away from home.

No one can stop me from seeing Bub. No one.

Saturday, October 2nd

"I am sorry to hear your family is so dead set against your happiness," said Bub in a calm voice as he lit a cigarette and watched the smoke swirling gracefully toward the ceiling of his candlelit room.

"But they don't want me to see you or help you or anything," I wailed. "I am only able to see you now because I got off Kowalski's early by telling him I had to run an errand for my father, which meant I could get home and have time to drop in without my father getting suspicious. Thank God I didn't run into him on the way up here. But if I had, I was going to tell him I was looking for him."

"A well-executed lie is one mark of a true gentleman," said Bub approvingly.

"But what will we do?" I cried. "You're my best friend!"

"Let me consult with my employer," replied Bub. "These situations can be tricky. He, wise soul that he is, shall know how to proceed. Leave it all to me."

"But they don't want me to help you tomorrow," I persisted. "They're making me take Grand to church."

Bud grimaced like he'd just taken a sip of vinegar or had eaten something nasty. "These people aren't even worth my attention," he muttered. Then, in a louder voice he said, "Do not worry, Vlad. This may turn out to be a blessing in disguise. I suspect this will be one of your final Sundays assisting your grandmother."

He didn't seem worried, but I am. Tomorrow's going to be the first day I can't help Bub and earn money. I could just not go to Grand's. But then I know my father would really lose it. I know he would. I'll just have to go to Grand's tomorrow and trust Bub when he says he'll figure something out. If anyone can figure something out, it's Bub.

And his boss sounds like a pretty cool guy, too. I'll just have to have faith in them.

Sunday, October 3rd

I'm back from church and lunch at Grand's, not that I had much appetite. I think Grand's been spending too much time praying and reading the Bible and talking to Father Kowalski and thinking about weird stuff she heard when she was a girl. Much too much time. It's affected her mind or something.

I don't even want to write down what she told me. About Bub, I mean. She's crazy, totally, 100% certifiably crazy. It's embarrassing. Maybe peasants in Poland believe that kind of stuff, but not people in New York City, not unless they're crazy. I never thought Grand was crazy, but maybe she's just gone crazy as she got older and I didn't notice it till now. I mean, that crazy stuff she was saying about Bub. She was saying he was— I can't even write it. It's too crazy.

Part of the time she was speaking to me in Polish, so maybe I didn't understand perfectly. If I had a good Polish/English dictionary I could be sure. And I could argue with her better, too. My Polish has gotten kind of rusty. I thought of stopping by the local library, but the woman who works there now is such a grouch. Last time I was there she yelled at me for no reason. Mrs. Manton, that was her name. I remember thinking she must be crazy—like Grand.

It's so crazy I can't stand it.

I was just coming in from school when I ran into Bub in the lobby. He looked very pleased to see me.

"What luck!" he said. "I just saw your father heading off on an errand—a hard-to-find part for my ceiling fan. You can drop in for a visit."

It felt good to be back in Bub's apartment. I'd been scared I might never see it again. Sometimes it seems like the nicest place on earth—much nicer than my dingy apartment or Grand's run-down little place. It's such a nice place it makes me think Grand must really have gone nuts. It's the kind of place I should live in. I deserve it. Bub thinks so, too.

"My employer is considering what to do next," Bub told me. "He is still waiting for certain, ah, up-to-date information. Then he shall advise us. His advice is never incorrect."

"Do you think he'll want me to start working for him soon?" I asked. "Then I could even move out of my father's and do exactly what I want to do."

"I think there's an excellent chance you might soon be in my employer's family, so to speak," said Bub.

"But . . . but aren't I maybe . . . kind of young?" I wondered.

"No. In fact, my employer has currently directed me to begin, ah, negotiations with a girl only a bit older than you—a high school senior, to be exact. Yes," he went on, half to himself, "we have high hopes for Becky Sue Anderson . . . For you, too," he added.

"All right!" I cheered, forgetting to act sophisticated.

"Oh," said Bub. "I was going through some books this morning, and happened upon this. I thought it might come in useful."

It was a Polish/English, English/Polish dictionary. And it looked new, too. Bub keeps his books in perfect shape. That's another sign of a real gentleman.

"How did you—" I began, then decided to act more nonchalant. "Thanks," I said. "This will come in handy."

"Yes," said Bub in sort of an absentminded tone, "it must be confusing sometimes, trying to make sense of what your grandmother says in her broken English and old-fashioned Polish."

"That's for sure."

"Sometimes, I imagine, she must use certain words or phrases that make you wonder if you heard her correctly, or perhaps misunderstood her altogether," Bub said.

"Yes," I had to agree. "Like yesterday! She said—"

Then I stopped. I couldn't say it out loud. Bub would hate me if I did. I know he would. He already seemed a bit preoccupied—he kept staring at me as if he was trying to guess what Grand had said, almost like he was trying to read my mind.

"What on earth could your grandmother have said to trouble you so?" he said, still examining my face.

"I . . . I don't want to say," I replied. "I better go," I blurted out, "before my father gets back."

I didn't care so much about my father. I was scared I might blurt out what Grand had said. And I didn't want to. Some things shouldn't be said, no matter what.

Wednesday, October 6th

Grand stopped in Kowalski's Locksmith Shop when I was working, right about when I was supposed to get off. She'd just left the church next door. I didn't feel like seeing her much, not after what she'd said on Sunday. And I'd understood her perfectly—I checked the word in the dictionary Bub gave me.

She was carrying two heavy bags filled with groceries, so I kind of had to help her get home—it's a long bus ride and then a walk up four steep flights of stairs. I know Bub says I should learn how to say no when people seem to think I'm only there to do them favors, but it's hard with Grand. Even if she does say crazy things sometimes.

Of course the second we were back in her apartment, she started talking crazy again. Except this time she was calmer. She kept pointing out different things. "You are smart boy," she'd say. "Think about what Grandmother is saying before deciding she is wrong."

So I did. All the way home, too. I still don't believe her—

I mean, this isn't the fourteenth century anymore, for God's sake—but I do kind of wonder. Some of the things she was saying do kind of add up a bit. Maybe it's a good thing not to see quite so much of Bub, at least until I figure things out a little. But it's still not fair—with the money I earn from Joe Kowalski, it'll take me years to save up enough for a computer. I'll never be able to compete with the snobs in my school, never. Juan says we're already dead ducks. And not seeing Bub would mean no more fancy clothes. I'm not sure seeing less of Bub is a good idea after all. Maybe I just need time to keep on thinking, just a few days.

Thursday, October 7th

I was in the elevator, coming down from the ninth floor, where my father'd had me deliver a UPS parcel to this couple in 9-K. They tipped me a quarter. Big deal.

The elevator stopped on the ground floor, on the way to the basement, and who should step in but Bub. I was sort of wishing I'd taken the service elevator, the way I'm supposed to, even though Bub says I shouldn't act like a second-class citizen even if my father is only a super.

Bub gave a cool smile to see me, like he knew I'd been avoiding him.

"Just the person I was hoping to see," he said, continuing to smile.

"Hi, Bub," I said slowly. I still didn't know what to think.

"Do you have a minute?" he asked.

"I guess so."

Bub led me to his apartment. A large box was sitting on his dining room table. At first I thought he'd gotten some new china he wanted me to help him unpack, but then he instructed me to look inside.

"But what's this for?" I asked, surprised.

"My employer is anxious for me to test out a new model," Bub explained, referring to the high-tech computer in the large box. "So much of my work these days is done over the Internet. Anyway, that means," he said, smiling again, "that as soon as I hook up the new machine and get it online, my current model is yours."

"For free?" I gasped by mistake.

"Vladimir," said Bub in a low voice, "nothing in life is free. But some things are worth the price."

I looked at Bub. He looked at me.

At that exact moment I knew Grand was right. Don't ask me how, but I knew. It was the most awful moment in my life, after the day Mother died.

I couldn't look at him anymore.

I ran.

Saturday, October 9th

I was coming home from Kowalski's, walking to save the subway fare. I was thinking about Bub. I was thinking about

Bub's computer. I was thinking about school. It was easier thinking about school than about Bub. Not better, but easier. Our English teacher had assigned work that *had* to be done on a computer. That meant waiting after school until one of the school's computers was free. But I had to go to Kowalski's dumb locksmith shop to earn slave wages, so I couldn't do the assignment as well as I wanted, and English is supposed to be my best subject. Every class is supposed to be my best subject, or so says the guidance counselor, if I want to get a scholarship to any decent college. I have to get straight A's. And how can I get an A in English if my assignments aren't great? I need that computer. I deserve it.

And Grand was right about something else. *If* she was right about Bub, that is. I'm starting to wonder. Maybe her craziness is catching. Anyway, what she was definitely right about is that I am starting to fill out all of a sudden. "Vlad is having growing spurt," she said proudly this morning when she stopped by Kowalski's again, doing yet another favor for that lazy Father Kowalski. He should embroider his own cushions.

I know I always wanted to fill out and get taller, but this is bad timing. Grand says her brother who died in the War grew six inches in two months when he was around my age. Great. I finally get a decent wardrobe and in six months it won't fit me anymore. And what if I never get more from Bub? I must have been wrong about what I thought. Maybe it was some kind of panic attack—I've read about them.

I saw him today, right when I was getting home, feeling

tired and poor and unhappy. He and Bella were leaving the building, all dressed up and smiling. They didn't get into a cab—they had a limo waiting for them. Bella threw me a kiss. I kind of waved back. I didn't know what to do. Bub nodded. He must think I'm crazy, running out of his apartment like that.

I watched the limo as it rolled down the street. It was a Rolls-Royce, I think. I watched until I rounded Gramercy Park and passed out of sight. It was like watching my future drive away without me. All my dreams—gone. I'll never get them back. It hurt so much I was scared I would cry. I didn't care anymore about what Grand said. Even if it is true, which I don't believe anymore. I was just standing there, trying to keep the tears in my eyes from falling down my cheeks. Then I heard my father start bellowing from the front door: "Vlad, get lazy ass in building and help me mopping floors now."

I don't know why, but that made me start to cry.

I didn't want my father seeing me cry, he'd just tease me or hit me. I didn't want anyone seeing me cry.

I couldn't help it, I just started running down the street as fast as I could, not tired anymore, running like a deer through a forest, running till I couldn't run anymore, like I was running for my life—running away, away from my father and the basement and the mopping and the Kowalskis and everybody who wants to keep me down and a nobody until I get old and die and never accomplish anything ever.

I ran and ran and ran.

Sunday, October 10th

"I am sure you won't mind sweeping out the church and washing the windows on the afternoons you work at my brother's."

That's what Father Kowalski said to me when Grand and I were leaving church today.

"Vlad is glad to be helping church," put in Grand before I could even speak.

What do they think I am—their personal slave? It's not enough I have to work for $3 an hour, now they want to get extra work out of me. And for no pay, too.

I'd even thought for a second about asking Father Kowalski about Bub. After all, he *is* a priest—they're supposed to know something. But all he knows about is how to get free work out of me. So forget asking *him* anything. They're all slave drivers. Grand, too. I'm not going to talk to her about it again, either.

I hate them all, even Grand. They've never done anything for me, not the way Bub has.

Bub. I don't think Grand's right after all, I think she's just jealous. That's why she said all that stuff. I let it get to me. I overreacted. I hope Bub can forgive me. I want my new life back—the money, the clothes, the new computer. Maybe even a ride in a Rolls-Royce. I hope Bub hasn't told his boss bad stuff about me.

Monday, October 11th

"Vladimir, is that you?" called Bub as I knocked on his door. He already knew it was me before I even said anything. It's like he really knows me through and through.

"I was expecting you," said Bub, placing a strong hand on my shoulder and ushering me back into his apartment, where a few candles were already burning, back into the candlelit room, back to where I belonged.

We sat side by side on the sofa.

My heart was in my mouth. My throat felt so small I wasn't sure I'd even be able to speak. But I had to. I had to make things right between Bub and me.

"Bub," I started, "I'm sorry. I got confused. It was what my grandmother said. I don't know why I listened to her in the first place. She's just an old lady who—"

But Bub interrupted me. He put his left hand on my shoulder and then turned my head with his right hand so we were looking in each other's eyes. For a moment no one spoke. Then Bub broke the silence.

"Your grandmother is quite correct."

"She . . . she can't be—"

"She is."

Then Bub caught me in his gaze and I looked deep into his eyes, just as he was looking into mine.

It was wonderful.

In Bub's eyes I saw everything I'd ever wanted. It was like watching a movie and I was the star. I was a bit older, dressed all fancy, opening the door to my penthouse. A beautiful woman was waiting for me, also a big staff of servants. My pockets were full of money—I could tell because my wallet was so thick.

Bub smiled and the movie ended.

"All you desire could be yours, Vlad," Bub said softly. "I can make it so, with the guidance of my gracious employer. But I cannot do it unless you agree. It is all up to you. Are you content to remain in a basement, just dreaming about a penthouse—or do you want to actually move to the penthouse? Because you can—with my help, you can do anything you want. Anything."

Bub then took my arm and led me to the hallway leading to his bedroom, the hall where all the red-framed photographs were. There definitely were more than the last time I looked. And now that I was looking more carefully, I thought I recognized a few famous faces—politicians and rock stars, that kind of famous. I also saw Mr. Harrison—so that was why he'd looked familiar.

"All these people have traded with me," explained Bub. "And now, thanks to my employer, who is the soul of generosity, each one is successful beyond his or her wildest dreams. So could you be, Vlad—so could you."

I kind of liked the idea of being on Bub's wall, of being

part of his family. His family was made up of rich and successful people. Mine consisted of a tired building super and an old lady.

"But . . . but why does everybody always say such . . . such terrible things about you?" I had to ask.

"That question has always intrigued me," Bub replied thoughtfully. "After much consideration, I have decided it is a combination of jealousy and ignorance. Also misinformation—many lies have been told about us. Unbelievable lies when you stop to think about them—yet so few people stop to think. Your father and grandmother, for example. They believe what they've been told without stopping to analyze. Just look where that's left them. It might be enough for *them*—but not for you. *You* deserve better, don't you?"

I do. I looked at Bub and smiled. He smiled back.

"I knew you were an intelligent young man," he said.

"Wh-what do I have to do?" I asked.

"My employer will draw up the contract, you sign, and—save for one detail—the transaction will be complete."

"And what's that?"

Bub led me back to the sofa and we sat down.

"A show of faith," he told me. "My employer, unfairly persecuted as he already is, wants no doubters in his following. You can understand why—our enemies are everywhere. Thus, before the contract is signed and we give you your dreams and you merely give us your—well, you know what . . . Utterly useless and highly overrated, too, that's what the soul is. At any rate, before this transaction is done, each individual undergoing confirmation into our family must perform some slight task that will indicate his allegiance to our side, a milestone if you will, from which there can be no turning back. A bridge from *their* side to *our* side."

I started to get nervous. What if they asked me to kill someone? I could never do that in a million years. Or maybe they'd ask me to rip up Mother's photograph. I couldn't do that, either.

"Wh-what will it have to be?" I asked.

Bub smiled before answering.

"Nothing *too* difficult," he reassured me. "Something symbolic of your decision. I shall have to consult with my employer, all-knowing benefactor that he is. Return on Wednesday and I shall let you know. Now, to toast your new life, the life you deserve, how about some wine?"

The red wine gave me courage and made me feel proud. Bub gave me a whole glass and he toasted me before each swallow. I'd never seen him so happy.

Tuesday, October 12th

School was bad today. I got my English paper back. A B−. I could have gotten an A if I'd had more time on the school computer. Or my own. But all that will change soon. Bub's new computer was still on the table—he hadn't installed it yet. That means when he does, his old model is mine! And it's ten times better than anything any of my dumb school-mates have. I'll run circles around them. Thanks to Bub.

And he's right about the soul part. I'm sure he is. It's only a word. You can't see it. And you sure can see computers and limos and fancy clothing and beautiful women. And other people can see them, too. I'll impress everyone.

And after school I had to put up with dumb Joe Kowalski and his fat brother. He wanted me to work on Tuesday and Thursday this week instead of Wednesday and Friday. And he seemed to want extra work out of me, too. First sweep the store and oil the machines, then sweep the church, then back to the store to run errands for Joe K., then back to the church to run errands for Father K. He should run his own errands, he might lose some weight. I don't know which I hate more—the locksmith shop or the dingy church. The locksmith shop smells of oil and machines and metal. The church smells of mold and dust and damp. That's what you get when you turn an old clothing goods store into a church (that's what Grand told me it used to be).

About the soul again. I was thinking of Mother. Everyone always said she had the most beautiful soul, that it shone right through her eyes and lit her way in life. And she did have a real glow, I can remember it. But if it was her soul, just look where it got her—a life of poverty in a dark basement and then a slow, painful death from cancer. She died because we're poor, I know she did. She was feeling bad for a long time, but wouldn't go to the doctor because it cost so much. She never let on how sick she felt. Then, when she did, it was too late. All the doctors kept saying if only she'd come earlier they could have saved her. Of course none of them would have seen her for free. So that's where her soul got her. I'm not going to end up like that. Bub won't let me.

But I do kind of wonder. I mean, Mr. Harrison didn't look too happy. Maybe some people just aren't made for success. But I think right after school tomorrow I'm going to stop by his store and see if I can speak with him in private.

Another annoying thing happened today. I was just leaving to go home with my big $12 when the phone rang. It was Grand. For me. That was weird. She could have called me at home.

"Vladski," she said, her voice breaking.

"What is it?"

"I am taking walk and am falling down."

"Are you hurt?" I asked, starting to get worried.

"Not hurt but clumsy."

"What do you mean?" I asked.

"I am falling on glasses and am breaking them. For reading I am needing them. I cannot be reading Bible before am sleeping. Vladski, I am hating to ask you, but could I be borrowing money to have glasses repaired? Am needing new frames. I will be paying you back on first of month."

So there goes $45 of my savings. I didn't mind as much as I might have, because I knew once Bub and I started working together I'd have money coming out my ears. I could buy Grand seven pairs of glasses, one for each day of the week.

"Okay, Grand," I said. "I have an errand to run after school tomorrow, then I'll bring you the money."

Tomorrow. My big day. My meeting with Bub. I get nervous just thinking about it.

Wednesday, October 13th—afternoon

To Mr. Harrison's after school. I ran all the way and got there around 3:30. I looked up and down the crowded sidewalk. Somehow I didn't want anyone to see me there. I also felt kind of nervous about going in, but I wanted to ask Mr. Harrison why he looked so unhappy. So I stood there a second, getting my courage up. I'm glad I waited—I was just about to head down the sidewalk and go in when who should come out the door of Mr. Harrison's but Bella. She had a big box in her arms and a pleased expression on her pretty face. I bet she just bought a nice present for Bub. Once she'd gone I walked up to the store. I was about to enter when I saw Mr. Harrison through the window. The place was busy as usual. And, unlike last time, Mr. Harrison had a big smile on his face. He must just have been in a bad mood last time. I decided not to go in and headed for Grand's.

When I'd dropped off the money, she asked me to take

her to the optometrist after school tomorrow—she'd made an appointment. I said okay.

I didn't tell her anything about Bub and, well, about what happened. I was sort of scared she'd worm it out of me. Even without her glasses she's pretty clear-sighted. But I'm smarter than she is. Better, too.

Wednesday, October 13th—evening

It's late and I'm just back from Bub's. I told my father I was taking a walk with Juan. Lying to him is like stealing candy from a big baby. I'm getting better at it by the day. Lying, that is. Bub says that it will come in handy later. Like tomorrow.

Here's what Bub wants me to do: rob Joe Kowalski's store. When I go to work next, I should copy the key to the back door, the one that goes into the alley. Then, that night, I sneak in and steal all the money from the cash register. On the way out I should smash the front door so it looks like a real robbery. Bub says this shouldn't be too hard—it's more like Kowalski owes me the money. He does, after paying me only $3 per hour.

The only tricky part is I have to leave some sort of clue that indicates it *might* have been me who'd done it. Not enough of a clue to get me arrested, but enough of one to make Joe Kowalski wonder enough to decide to let me go. Bub says he wouldn't accuse me outright, but would just make up some excuse why he didn't need me anymore.

"I told you you wouldn't be stuck too long at Kowalski's Locksmith Shop," Bub said, smiling.

I work again on Friday after all, since tomorrow I was given off to take Grand to the optometrist.

I'm kind of scared. Nervous. I know that maybe it's not right, no matter how big a slave driver Joe K. is. But then maybe it is. If he weren't so unfair to me, then I'd find someone else to rob. Anyway, Bub says it will all be worth it in the long run. And he must be right. Just look at how he lives.

Wednesday, October 13th—evening, later on

Uh-oh. Grand just called. She'd gone to church for evening mass, and ran into Joe K. Now he says he wants me to work tomorrow *after* I take Grand to the eye doctor's. He has to move some machines or something. Great. That means I can get the key copied. That means tomorrow night is the robbery. One minute I think I don't want to go through with it. Then the next minute I think of what my life would be like if I don't—no Bub, no computer, no money, no nothing. I have to do it. And it must mean something that Bub moved into *my* building. We were meant to meet. This was all meant to happen. It must have been.

.   .   .

"Vladimir, where is the money?" asked Bub. "My employer always demands proof."

I bowed my head. I didn't want to look Bub in the eye.

"I didn't do it," I had to admit.

"My employer will be very disappointed to hear this," said Bub in kind of a cold voice.

"I just . . . I just . . . just didn't," I stammered.

"Did you copy the key to the back door?"

"Yes," I said in a firmer voice. "That's all ready."

"My employer, patient soul that he is, is not accustomed to being kept waiting," intoned Bub.

I took a deep breath.

"It was the book," I said. "I'd decided to leave one of my schoolbooks behind during the robbery. That would point suspicion toward me, but it wouldn't be conclusive proof."

"Good thinking," said Bub, nodding his head. "So what happened?"

"I . . . I left the book at home. And," I confessed, "I was also pretty nervous."

"The nervous heart will never attain greatness," Bub told me, his gaze sweeping around his beautifully appointed apartment. "Never."

I took another deep breath.

"Bub," I said, "maybe if you . . . if you came with me, I . . . I could do it."

"That is most irregular."

"Please, Bub, I want you there. It would mean a lot to me. I'd do all the unlocking of doors and all that stuff. You'd . . . you'd just be there. I'd feel better that way. I need you to be there."

Bub inhaled, then reached out for my chin, raising my head so he was looking in my eyes. He arched an elegant eyebrow as he continued examining my face. I tried hard to meet his gaze, keeping my mind clear and strong so Bub wouldn't doubt me. I want to make him believe me, to trust in me. I'm sick of this life I'm living, really sick. No one knows how sick of it I am.

"You are speaking the truth?" asked Bub, still staring.

"Yes, Bub. It's true when I say it would mean a lot to me to have you there."

"Tomorrow night then. After midnight," said Bub finally. "It will give me great pleasure to watch this act done on what by then will be Sunday morning."

Saturday, October 16th

Another long day at Joe K.'s. Of course I was thinking about other things. I was busy, too—sweeping and polishing and you name it. But soon I'll be free of all this—all this hard stuff. At least, I hope so. As Bub says, you can't even see the soul, so what's the big deal? He says you get rid of something you hardly know you have and you get the world in return.

I don't want to write anymore. I'm pretty nervous. I think I'll just lie down and pretend it's all over. If I can do it, that is. I don't mean if I can pretend, I mean if I can do *it*.

Saturday, October 16th—later on

I can't sleep. I'm wondering even more if I can do it, wondering so much that I had to get out of bed and write some more. Can I do it? I think I can. I have to be strong. Should I do it? It's the right thing to do, that's what I keep telling myself, no matter how many doubts I have. I feel so close to Bub, like he's a real friend. That doesn't make it easier. But I know my whole future depends on it. It's too late to back out now. I've got to see it through. I can do it. I know I can do it. I'm not just some skinny little Polish nobody who lives in a basement. I'm more than that. I know I am. I am. I am. I am.

Sunday, October 17th

I did it. I succeeded. My future is going to be great. I knew I could do it. I knew it, I really did.

Here's what happened:

I got into bed with my clothes on to save time later. But then I couldn't sleep. That's when I got up again and wrote a bit more in my diary. Just a few lines, but it seemed to settle my thoughts. Or my nerves. Whatever. Then I lay down again. I didn't even try to sleep, I just lay there, sort of resting.

After a while I heard my father grunt the way he does when he lays his tired body down into bed, kind of like a pig squirming around in its sty, looking for a comfortable position. He always falls asleep quickly. I can count to ten, and by then I hear him snoring. Loudly and irregularly—the most annoying way to snore, because you never know what's going to happen next, more snoring or a few moments of quiet.

So I waited, just to make sure my father was really asleep. Ten minutes of solid snores convinced me. I checked my clock: 11:37. For some reason I decided to wait until 11:40 exactly. Then I got up. Carrying my shoes, I tiptoed out of the apartment, taking the copied keys and the book with me. Outside the door I put on my shoes and took the stairs up to the fourth floor. I didn't want to meet anyone in the elevator. Even the service elevator seemed too risky—once in a while a tenant uses it, when they get impatient waiting for the regular one. They might wonder where I was going, all dressed in black, at around midnight.

Before I even knocked, Bub was at the door, ready. He, too, was dressed in black, except for a red tie that looked like it was made of silk, and rippled like a flame when you changed angles.

He put a finger to his lips, indicating we should keep quiet. That was fine with me. Then he pointed toward me, then toward the stairs. He pointed to himself, then toward the elevator.

I guess it wouldn't do to be seen leaving the building together. People might wonder or talk and I didn't want that.

We reconnoitred outside and started walking. Once we'd turned the corner at the end of the block, we started talking. It was kind of a relief, I guess.

Bub turned to me and smiled. "This is an important moment," he said. "I am honored to be witnessing it, unusual as it might be. I am grateful that my employer—soon to be your employer as well—consented despite his misgivings and permitted it. I feel a special bond with you, like father and son."

I bowed my head.

"There is no need to be humble," said Bub. "You were right about yourself: you are more than some skinny little kid. Much more."

I nodded. "I know," I said finally. "I am."

Although it was past midnight, the streets were still pretty filled with people. It was a warm night for mid-October, and a Saturday night, too. Lots of people passed us. Luckily no one seemed to notice us. Maybe the black clothes helped make us less obvious, I don't know. Usually Bub is quite striking-looking, the kind of person passersby notice.

"I remember my first time," said Bub dreamily as we walked north up the avenue. I understood without Bub having said it that we would walk to Kowalski's Locksmith Shop. A taxi was too risky—we might be remembered by the driver. And somehow I couldn't imagine Bub taking the subway. "Yes," continued Bub, "my first time."

I wasn't sure if he meant the first time he'd performed an act to show his good faith, or the first time he'd worked with someone who was performing *his* show of good faith.

"It was ages ago," Bub went on as the sidewalks started getting emptier. "Ages." I glanced up at his face and noticed a strange faraway look in his eyes. I wondered how old he was. From the way he was speaking, he could be talking about something that happened centuries ago.

"Abraham Lincoln was in the White House," he continued, almost as if he'd read my mind. "At least for the moment."

"Abraham Lincoln!" I couldn't help but gasp. I was trying not to lose my cool.

"My job was more interesting then. The lines were etched harder between the two camps—people were more loath to cross. I enjoyed the challenge. And once they did, we could expect more out of them—not today's penny-ante nonsense. Johnny Booth—beginner's luck on my part, I suppose. But modern times have their compensations," he added, almost as if he'd forgotten I was there. "An innocent soul like yours, for example, makes my job that much more rewarding."

I bowed my head. I wasn't feeling that innocent. I also wasn't quite sure what Bub was talking about, anyway.

The keys were feeling heavy in my pocket, like boulders. The book felt like a boulder in my hand. I was trying to keep my mind a blank, so I wouldn't chicken out. Thinking seemed dangerous—I would just start coming up with reasons why it wouldn't work. And I didn't want Bub to know what I was feeling. I wanted him to be confident in me.

We lapsed into silence for a while. The only sounds were the passing cars and buses, our footsteps, and the keys jangling in my pocket—louder and louder, louder and louder.

"You can't do it, you can't do it"—that's what they seemed to be saying.

Then I felt Bub looking at me, looking hard.

"You are having doubts?" he asked.

I took a deep breath. "A bit," I said, still trying to keep my mind a blank, to keep the doubting thoughts away.

"So did I, my first night. All doubts pass. Trust me."

I bowed my head again, watching my shoes passing like black shadows above the gray of the sidewalk.

"Step on a crack, break your mother's back." That old rhyme came into my head. If I didn't step on a crack the rest of the way, everything would be all right. I began walking more carefully, avoiding the cracks.

I felt Bub staring at me again. I looked over at him as we walked.

"I love superstitions," he remarked. "They are often helpful in my line of work."

I nodded, still avoiding the cracks.

Then we arrived. There was Kowalski's Locksmith Shop, dark and silent, a "Closed, Please Come Again" sign hanging in the front door.

Slowly, quietly, we made our way up the street, around the corner, and into the alley behind the store. It was even darker than the street—quieter, too. Spooky.

Bub produced a flashlight and handed it to me.

I took another deep breath. I wasn't sure anymore if I could do it. I knew I wanted to. I had to. I just wasn't sure I could.

I felt sick to my stomach. I breathed again, deeply, trying to calm myself.

"Don't think about it, don't think about it," I kept repeating to myself. "Don't think about it, don't think about it."

My hand was shaking so hard when I trained the flashlight on the small handwritten sign taped on the back door—the sign saying "Kowalski's Locksmith Shop, Service Entrance"—that it was hard to read it. But I noticed Bub's eyes narrowing thoughtfully as he scanned it. Then he gave a nod as I pulled out the keys. Still shaking violently, I managed to unlock the door, first one lock, then another, then the third. One by one I heard the bolts slide, then the slight shudder as the old door loosened somewhat. Soon there would be no turning back.

"Don't think about it, don't think, don't think, don't think," I kept repeating, like a prayer, like a mantra, like the Pledge of Allegiance. "Don't think about it. Just do it. Just do it. Just do it."

"What are you thinking about?" asked Bub unexpectedly, peering at me in the darkness.

"About just doing it," I said, my voice shaking.

"Good," said Bub. "I would have known the feel of a lie. Just doing it is all you need to think about."

The door opened and I switched off the flashlight.

"I don't want anyone to see," I said quietly.

"Very wise," said Bub, still staring at me intently, looking through the darkness for—for what? What was he looking for? Was he finding it?

I held the door open wide, my arm trembling so much I thought I might just fall over or start crying.

"Don't think about it, just do it. Do it. Do it," I kept repeating inside my head.

"Vlad," said Bub in a gentle voice, staring at me hard. "What *are* you thinking?"

I took a deep breath, then another.

I held the door open.

"I was thinking about just doing it. Now I'm thinking it would be nice if you went in first. I want to follow you."

"Follow me you shall," said Bub, stepping past me, through the door, into the darkness, into the silence inside.

It wasn't silent for long.

The moment Bub stepped in he gave a horrible shriek, a shriek of pain and anger and surprise. The very next moment the linoleum tiles on the floor totally vanished. Now Bub was standing not on the floor but on solid darkness, darkness that echoed beneath him as he screamed. For a second I could see the darkness—it was actually there. Like it was solid. It even smelled—a sickly, sulfurous smell, nauseating. It was like an elevator shaft into the earth, a shaft that never seemed to stop. The next moment, as Bub still seemed to hover over the shaft of darkness, clutching at the air, reaching for the walls that were just beyond his grasp, he managed to twist around and face me. His face was distorted with rage, livid with anger, almost unrecognizable. His eyes were slits of blood-red fury and his mouth was a gash across his face, his teeth suddenly pointier and stained. And he was ugly—the ugliest person I'd ever seen. For a second I thought maybe it wasn't even Bub—that's how different he looked. With a lunge, he reached his arms out for me, his arms that seemed to stretch like tentacles as they reached for me. Even his fingernails were changed—somehow in the darkness I could see they'd become pointed and filthy. And sharp, too. I jumped back when he reached—but not quite quickly enough. They tore through my shirt, ripping it into shreds. But he couldn't grab me, I was an inch too far away. And he was somehow trapped there in space.

His mouth opened wide and this horrible snakelike tongue came darting out, flapping in fury, in pain, in shock. It was a dark, blood-red color, not like a human tongue.

He spoke one word—my name.

"Vladimir!" he cried.

Then, suddenly, I realized why I'd been able to see—the blackness had been steadily lessening. Soon I saw why. Out of the shaft burst a tongue of flame, flame so hot I had to leap back even further in order not to get singed. I watched in horror as Bub was enveloped in it, floating like an ember above a fire. Part after part of his body burst into flame and kept on burning. He was writhing in pain, screaming in a language I couldn't understand. And the fire kept on burning him, but he didn't seem to burn up. The fire kept raging, the flesh kept burning. It seemed as though Bub would burn for ever and ever and it would never stop hurting, never ever.

He gave one last look in my direction, a look of unspeakable pain, of unfathomable anger, a look of pure and eternal hatred.

Then came a noise like an immense vacuum, a whoosh of foul wind, and Bub was sucked down into the shaft, vanishing down, down, down, out of sight. The flame flared a second, then died down, like it was following Bub down the shaft.

Then both were gone, Bub and the flame. In the blink of an eye, the floor reappeared, none the worse for having a fire just burning in its midst. I checked with my flashlight. There wasn't even a mark on the walls, nothing to indicate what had just happened there.

I took another deep breath and crossed myself.

Then I shut the door and locked it. I thought the metal felt a bit warm, but that might only have been my imagination.

The last thing I did, before leaving, was to remove the handwritten sign saying "Kowalski's Locksmith Shop, Service Entrance."

I had the right to remove it—I had put it there in the first place.

Once it was gone, you could read what was there to begin with. Stenciled onto the metal door, in small block letters, were the words "Polish American Church, Deliveries Only."

I didn't go home. I went to Grand's. She was waiting for me.

Monday, October 18th

I didn't go to school today. I was too tired. Grand called up and said I was ill. Actually I wasn't sick. I was better. Really better.

She called my father, too, in case he noticed I wasn't there this morning.

Here's what happened. I've got to write it down, otherwise I'll keep on reliving it in my head, like a weird nightmare, like a scary movie. Maybe by writing it down I can move ahead, move on, move up, much more easily. I hope so. But of course the main thing is I did it. Me. Vladimir Mikula. I did it. I really did.

A while back I realized that Bub had special powers. Psychic powers. Like whatever I wrote in my diary, he knew about it. He was sort of a mind reader, and he was focusing his powers on me. And if I thought something *and* put it down on paper, too, that was enough for him to know exactly what I'd written. He also did a pretty good job of reading minds just by looking at me. But he wasn't perfect—like when he thought I was *embarrassed* when he gave me those wool pants. I wasn't embarrassed by the gift, just upset because I couldn't wear them. And he only knew I'd admired them in the first place because he knew I'd written about them in my diary.

When I knew what he was, when I really knew, once I'd accepted the fact, I have to admit something. I've told Grand, but I'm never going to tell anyone else. But I want to write it down. Here it is. I really was ready to sell my soul. I really was. It seemed worth it to get all those things. Thank God I didn't. Now that I've seen a glimpse of Hell, that is.

It was Grand who helped me think it through. It wasn't that she told me what to do—she just helped me to see what it was I really wanted to do, deep inside. I didn't write about that in the diary. Grand told me not to. With her questioning, I realized how Bub could read my thoughts when I wrote them down. I guess he flubbed up a bit—like when he suddenly knew Forrest Carrington's and Skip Basingwell's last names. I'd never told him. But I had written them down. So I started using my diary to trick Bub. All that about Grand's glasses was a lie—she made it up so we could spend time together without making Bub suspicious. But I never knew it was a lie until later—when I wrote about it in my diary I still thought it was true. Grand explained how I could bend the truth in my diary, but never break it. Bub was right—he did know the feel of a lie. After all, he'd had enough experience with lying. Anyway, that's why I skipped October 14th in my diary—I was getting my head together. From then on, everything I wrote was a camouflage of the truth. It wasn't easy. But Bub believed it. Just like I believed all that stuff he told me. I really did. That's what made it so hard to give it all up. And

I liked Bub, too. I really did. It was the most difficult decision I've ever had to make.

And it was a decision I had to make myself.

It was harder than anyone will ever know. It meant giving up a lot. But a soul is more important. And I sort of think that part of Mother's soul is in me. I couldn't sell her soul, I just couldn't.

Once I'd made my decision, it was Grand who knew how to get rid of a devil. It was something she'd remembered hearing about when she was a girl—about a church being the only place on earth a devil can't go. And if you trick one into setting foot in a church, they go straight back to Hell, and once they're back they're punished forever for messing up. And they can't come back to earth anymore to trade in souls. Grand says that for a devil, working on earth is kind of a cushy job.

So Grand came up with the idea. But I had to do it. I had to trick Bub into coming with me. And I had to avoid lying. A devil knows the smell of a lie. I think I was pretty clever in saying (and writing) things that weren't lies, but still didn't say exactly what Bub thought they did. I just reread my diary, and even I'm pretty impressed with myself. Maybe I'll be an actor when I grow up.

Or maybe not.

I have a lot of time to think about a career. I'm not sure I want a career that involves tricking people, the way I tricked Bub. It didn't feel good. And a little part of me misses him. I even feel a bit guilty—I can't forget the way he looked at me. Grand says that's normal. I wonder how long it will take the police to give up looking for him. I wonder if they'll question Bella. I wonder if she was one, too. I don't know what my career will be. Maybe I'll have lots of money, maybe I won't. It's funny, I'd still love to be rich, though as Grand says, "in life there are other things."

And now I know I'm determined. And strong. Stronger than I ever knew I was. Strong as Grand always said I was. Strong enough to resist Bub. I knew as we were approaching the church that Bub was getting stronger and stronger. I think maybe the fact that he was about to win over another soul swelled his psychic abilities. I don't know, but I could feel the difference. And he must have been feeling something different in me, too. Why else would he keep asking me what I was thinking? He'd never asked that before. I had to keep my thoughts my own. I had to stick to what I knew I had to do.

And I did it. Me, Vladimir Mikula. A skinny little Polish kid. Except now I'm less skinny and I don't feel little anymore. And I sure don't feel like a kid.

I just don't feel worried anymore about what's going to happen.

I figure if I can do this, I can do anything.

CARING

THE COLLEGE ADMISSIONS ESSAY
OF BECKY SUE ANDERSON

here are four main reasons why I feel sure I should be admitted to South Central University. I will summarize them here, then go into more depth in the ensuing paragraphs. First, like South Central itself, I too have an excellent academic reputation (I am, after all, the valedictorian of my class!). Second, I am a caring and dutiful daughter. As an only child, I take my responsibilities to heart, particularly when I recall the tragedies my parents have endured, namely the untimely deaths of my younger siblings. Third, as a vital and contributing member of society, I am deeply involved with various clubs and organizations, both in the school community and the community at large. But I don't stop there. I think charity begins at home, and I can be counted on to be a caring friend through good times and bad. Like with Eileen Kreckler, who was my dearest friend. And fourth, I am a young person with a deep respect for my elders. In summation to my introductory paragraph, I'd like to quote what my dear grandmother said about me. She said, "Becky Sue, if caring were a crime, they'd have to find you guilty!" Thank you, Grandma, for those kind words.

And before I begin my essay, I'd like to dedicate it to the loving memory of my grandmother, Elizabeth Ann Anderson. Despite her tragic passing earlier this year, I hope to honor her memory by doing well in college, my way of thanking Grandma for remembering me in her will and leaving me enough money to attend college as well as putting away a nice little nest egg for later on.

I am both proud of and humbled by my standing as class valedictorian. Having a straight "A" average isn't easy for a girl as busy and popular as I am. As Eileen used to say, somewhat enviously I thought, "Becky Sue, it's just not fair—you've got both looks *and* brains!" While that's certainly true, I feel my academic ability is even more important than my good looks, and I am confident it will come in useful when I pursue a career in the field of law or perhaps advertising. I am humble, though, because I know these gifts are God-given. Gifts, however, that I've worked hard to use. As Grandma used to say, "God helps those who help themselves." Truer words were never spoken.

I am humble, also, when I think of my dear friend, Eileen Kreckler. She and I were neck and neck to be named valedictorian in the middle of last term. I thought that we were *tied,* and how wonderful it was going to be to *share* this honor with such a decent, deserving girl as Eileen. I told her so, of course. Therefore Eileen's neighbor Anna, that mousy girl in our French class, just has to be mistaken when she claims she heard Eileen and me discussing our grades, and that Eileen told me she was sure *she* was going to be the sole valedictorian because she was expecting to get four "A+"s and one "A" while I was only expecting two "A+"s and three "A"s. I think Anna must have been confused—perhaps it's those hideous thick glasses she wears that make her look like some sort of trout. I can swear that Eileen and I *never* had such a conversation. That's where my modesty comes in. I'm proud of my good grades, but I refuse to discuss them in public with anyone, even poor Eileen. And if Eileen had been so sure she was going to be named valedictorian and have her name added to the bronze plaque in front of Ridgefield High and have that wrinkled old Mr. Leahy, the richest man in town, give her a congratulatory check for $1,000, then she would never have been so worried about her grades. And she *was* worried about her grades—really, *really* worried. I know this because Eileen shared her concerns with me one day not too long before it happened. This proves what a caring person I am—that Eileen chose *me* to confide in. She didn't tell anyone else, not even her parents or her minister or her scrawny neighbor Anna, the one with the bad memory. What Eileen confided was that she was simply in a panic about her grades, and the pressure of being up against me for class valedictorian was getting to be too much for her. She was afraid she would crack. After all, grades *were* about the only thing Eileen had. She certainly never had a date, much less a boyfriend! It wasn't her fault that she wasn't very pretty, but she wasn't. I'm just being truthful. Of course, an attempt at a diet might have proved useful, but Eileen *did* like to eat.

Anyway, Eileen told me how tense and hysterical she was feeling, although she'd been able to hide it from everyone thus far. She was even scared she might do something stupid. Then she begged me to tell no one—*no one!*—what she'd told me.

I promised I wouldn't tell, but that's one promise I broke. I felt I had to—that it was much more important to be caring. So I met privately with Mr. and Mrs. Kreckler. I told them what Eileen had told me. They were worried, of course, and said they would speak with her. But when they did, Eileen denied ever saying anything to me about her desperate feelings. Mrs. Kreckler was quite icy to me on the phone afterwards, suggesting I was perhaps mistaken, but saying it in a nasty sort of voice. I told her I was just trying to be a caring person, and hung up. I'm positive Mrs. Kreckler and Mr. Kreckler too (if you catch him in a sober moment) will always regret not believing me.

It happened only two days later. Eileen and I went into the City every Tuesday to take a college-level course so we'd be more prepared for our entry into college this autumn (just another example of how much I care about my academic career!). Well, it was on the way to class and we were both in the Ridgefield train station. I noticed Eileen make her way down to the far end of the platform (with her girth she was kind of hard *not* to notice!), where she stood all alone. At first I thought she was avoiding me, because of what I'd told her parents. I thought this because when she walked by me (I was standing in the middle of the platform) she had this weird expression on her face. But since I care about people, I kept an eye on her. She was *definitely* acting odd—she kept leaning over the platform, pretending she was looking for the train. But I didn't quite believe it. *I knew how upset she'd been, even if nobody believed me yet.*

It happened just as the train could be heard approaching the station. Eileen took a big step forward—right up to the edge of the platform—acting as though she wanted to be in place to board the train when it had pulled in and stopped. I wasn't fooled, though—that was when it struck me why she'd walked all the way down to the end of the platform where she could be all alone, and why she had such a weird expression on her face. I suddenly knew what she was going to do. I didn't waste a second. It's not for nothing I'm such a good cheerleader and so naturally athletic. I quickly threw down my books, not caring what happened to them—even though, as I have previously mentioned, academic achievement is *so* important to me—and raced down to the end of the platform. At first I thought I'd got there in time. Eileen was just getting ready to throw herself in front of the train which was about to enter the station. Witnesses from farther down the platform can attest to how we struggled. I don't mean to boast. I was only doing what anyone would have done—trying to save the life of a friend. We did indeed struggle. Eileen was no athlete, but she was a very big girl. Just when I thought I was going to be able to pull her back to safety, just when the train was rumbling into the station, Eileen somehow slipped out of my grasp and ended up over the edge of the platform, landing right in front of the train. It was a terrible moment when the train first hit her and then ran her over. Witnesses say I was very, very brave; that I hardly cried and was able to provide the police with all the pertinent information. I may have been calm on the *outside,* but *inside,* I was *very* upset, I can tell you that. That accounts for why I was unable to finish those two extra-credit reports I had due later that week, and why I ended up with only two "A+"s and not four. This didn't happen until *after* Eileen died, so that's just further evidence that that dwarf Anna was lying when she said all that stuff about grades. I mean, how could Eileen and I talk about something that hadn't even happened yet, I'd like to know. The teachers involved told me they'd give me extra time to pull my notes together and write the actual reports, but I said no. I don't believe in receiving preferential treatment. I want to be judged on what I do, not on what's happened to me. One teacher even offered to grade me just on my notes, but I also refused. Anyway, I was so upset by then that I'd thrown them out, that's why I didn't have any. They'd reminded me of what happened to Eileen because she was in the same class.

So, you can see, even though I was named valedictorian, it is a title I hold with some degree of humility. My grades speak for themselves, I know, with my "A" average, but perhaps my humility needs to be brought to your attention. That alone is why I mention all this about Eileen, not to boast about how nearly I was able to save her life. And I don't just mean in the train station—I also mean before, when I attempted to tell the Krecklers how upset Eileen was and they didn't listen to me. They were big enough to apologize to me afterwards, for not listening to me. I told them not to mention it again, because that's just the kind of caring person Becky Sue Anderson is. I also spent some of the $1,000 I received from old Mr. Leahy in sending a lovely, understated little bouquet in remembrance of Eileen to her parents with the sweetest note just to show there were no hard feelings.

My second qualification for being admitted to South Central is that in addition to being a dedicated student, I am also a dedicated daughter, always caring and kind. Mother and Father both say they would be lost without me, and it's not boasting to say it's true. Too many girls my age give their parents a hard time—but not Becky Sue Anderson. *I* don't wish to give my parents anything extra to worry about. There are a few reasons for this. First of all, both my parents have high-pressure jobs. They work together in a public relations firm they founded, Anderson Associates. For a while they did very well, but the last few years have been kind of rough. I know their loss of income has been very troubling to them, though they never mention it. After all, Mother's always been kind of high-strung—when she worries too much she tends to get ill. And Father has a history of ulcers. So that's why I don't want anyone or anything to worry them unnecessarily. And there's another reason, a sad one, which I want to share not to get sympathy but so the Admissions Board at South Central will know Becky Sue Anderson is a strong, caring girl who has faced tragedy and survived to keep on caring. What happened is this: When I was twelve, Mother gave birth to twins. Although no one admitted as much, I know it was an unplanned and unwanted pregnancy. After all, hadn't Mother *always* said, "My little Becky Sue is the perfect child. Why have more?" Also, both Mother and Father had little enough spare time for me as it was. And I could tell Father was terribly worried about the expense of raising two more children, although he was too proud to mention it. As it turned out, Father's unspoken economic fears were well founded. The twins were *incredibly* expensive. Both had a lot of health problems, due, I think, to their being premature. (It also didn't do much for their appearance. Most people, on seeing them, simply could not believe they were related to me. Not that this bothered me, of course—no matter how unfortunate their appearance was, they were still dear to me.) And needless to say, they required endless amounts of attention. Sure enough, starting with their birth, life changed around the Anderson house. For one thing, money became very tight. This did not trouble me, mind you—I am always glad to share. I never complained when my wardrobe budget was cut in half and my ski trip was cancelled and when Mother warned me we were going to have to cancel our membership in the Ridgefield Oaks Country Club, the *only* club worth belonging to, in my opinion. I didn't even complain when Mother said it looked like we'd have to scale down the huge graduation party I'd been planning since tenth grade. Anyway, none of this troubled me, but I *was* troubled to see how strained and ill at ease Mother was looking, although she bravely claimed she'd never felt happier. And once they became toddlers, they were not nearly as well behaved as they might have been. In fact, they were constantly naughty. I didn't mind so much on *my* account when they smashed my china horse collection into smithereens—I only worried because it worried Mother. Father too. I just knew his ulcers were acting up again—not that he would admit it, of course, not wishing to cause concern. And even though I wanted to go to France very badly the summer of my junior year—primarily to improve my French (not that it needed all that much improvement, what with my high "A—" average)—I didn't complain when Mother and Father said we simply could no longer afford such an extravagant holiday and instead would borrow this dinky little lakeside house belonging to one of their business associates, with this horrible steep path down to this scummy little lake that was always cold on account of being so deep. Mother says I've never been a complainer and that's true. I kept my mouth shut, too, even when I didn't get the red Mustang convertible I'd been promised for my seventeenth birthday ever since I was eight, just because the twins were so expensive. I was *so* looking forward to volunteering my time and Mustang to drive senior citizens back and forth to do their shopping! Well, it was rather ironic that the two who'd deprived me of *my* car (not to mention a decent wardrobe, a ski trip, a respectable country club membership, a party, *and* a trip to France) should love to play so much in Mother's, a light blue recent-model minivan. Perhaps they thought it was a little house, who knows? I of course informed Mother and Father I'd seen the twins playing in the minivan where Mother had parked it on the steep driveway at the summer house—or, to be more accurate, summer *hut,* not that this bothered me, I just thought Mother and Father deserved better. Well, the twins of course denied ever playing in the minivan, and even stuck out their plump pink tongues from between their embarrassingly protruding teeth, right in my direction. I didn't hold this against them—after all, they *were* only children and hadn't learned the difference between right and wrong. It's just sad that their lying led to what finally happened.

It was on a Sunday. Mother and Father were sitting in the living room, reading the paper. I was in my room on the side of the house, the ugly little room overlooking the driveway. (I of course had insisted the twins have the nicer bedroom.) I was reading a book that was on my English class's summer reading list. I was plowing through the book when I have to admit I fell asleep, partially because I was bored and partially because it was such a hot, muggy morning. Well, perhaps I *am* a little bit psychic—Grandma always said there was more to me than meets the eye!—but I awoke from my sleep with a start. For no reason, I had the most dreadful thought that the twins were in trouble. I ran into the living room and asked Mother and Father if they'd seen them. Mother said no, not since breakfast. I suggested Mother check their room and Father check the basement. I volunteered to check around the house. Father came out of the basement a few minutes later, but it was already too late. He saw me running heroically after the minivan, which was speeding down the driveway, trying vainly to catch up with it and jump inside and stop it. (I should add that we could spot the twins inside, seeming to enjoy the ride.) But the van was rolling too quickly and the driveway was too steep. Helplessly we watched as the minivan careened down the driveway, crashed through the hedge at the bottom, and plunged into the lake beneath with a big splash. It sank in less than ninety seconds and the lake was too deep for me to dive in and rescue them, even though I tried. Father says I was very valiant, diving in again and again all by myself, telling him to call for help instead of diving in because I was concerned about him overexerting himself. But it was all no use. According to the coroner, the twins had somehow disengaged the parking brake and put the van into neutral, although no one was sure how this had been accomplished or why they'd put their seat belts on. Mother and Father were dreadfully upset, as was I, only I didn't like to show it, not wishing to add to Mother and Father's distress. Mother says it was only my kind thoughtfulness and caring that got them through this tragedy. But that's just the kind of person I am—caring and thoughtful—and that's why I feel I would be such an important asset to South Central.

Thirdly, I'd like to share some of the things I've done in the community, both the school community and the community at large. I feel community involvement is very vital and I do more than just talk about it. Among the school clubs I'm a member of are: Cheerleading Club, the French Club, Future Lawyers of America Club, Young Republicans Club, and the Student Council (Treasurer). In terms of the community at large, I am a former candy striper and a member of The Visitors, a bunch of teens who visit senior citizens confined to hospitals and old-age homes. But, like I said at the beginning of this essay, charity begins at home, and I also found time to visit my grandmother, Elizabeth Ann Anderson, at least twice a week in the small apartment she'd moved to after a stroke forced her to leave her lovely old house with the extensive property (three and one quarter acres of prime real estate). She had a visiting nurse who helped out six hours a day by the name of Charlotte. Grandma loved Charlotte so much she was even planning to change her will to leave her a surprisingly large amount of money. I wasn't so sure about the wisdom of this—and *not* because it meant I would inherit less. It was because I thought Charlotte was careless and had told her so. I came over more than once and found she'd put a thick plastic mattress cover on Grandma's bed, beneath the sheets. I knew she'd done this to save herself time in case Grandma had an accident during the night, but I didn't think this was right. I'd learned from my volunteer work as a candy striper that plastic mattress covers can be dangerous for both babies and ill, weak older people. A nurse had explained that if the cloth sheets become displaced, the baby or older person can end up facedown against the plastic, and if it's a warm night and they sweat a lot, or if they drool, then the moisture can form something like a seal, and they can suffocate. It's rare, but it does happen. I instructed Charlotte never to use plastic mattress covers again and she became incensed, claiming she'd never used one in the first place. I don't think very much of liars and told her so. Of course I informed Father (it was his mother), and he had a word with Charlotte. Once again she denied using plastic mattress covers. Father doesn't think much of liars either, especially when he found a plastic mattress cover crammed in a closet at Grandma's apartment. Charlotte swore up and down that she'd never seen it before, but I don't think anyone believed her. Charlotte was always very cold to me after that whenever I visited Grandma, but I don't hold it against her. I didn't tell on her to get her in trouble, but to help her do her job better and to show I cared. I knew it might make things uncomfortable, but I felt it was more important to do the right thing—the caring thing, the community-minded thing. That's what makes what happened so especially tragic—it didn't have to happen, not if Charlotte had listened to me.

I visited Grandma one night last September when we

were in the midst of an Indian summer. It was after Charlotte had left for the night, and I wanted to make sure Grandma had had dinner and would get to bed all right. Grandma was weak, but she could still get around a bit. Mother says it was just like me, to give up a date on a Friday night to spend time with Grandma. When she'd finished watching her TV program (which I didn't watch as I didn't care for its tone) I escorted Grandma to her bedroom, where I put her to bed and kissed her good-night as usual, even though I don't particularly care for the way old people smell. I don't hold it against them of course, I just thought I'd mention it in passing.

It so happened that the following morning I realized I'd left my Calculus notebook at Grandma's and went over early to pick it up, before that untruthful Charlotte showed up for work. If only I'd arrived a bit earlier! When I'd put Grandma to bed the night before, I somehow hadn't noticed that that lazy Charlotte had sneaked the plastic mattress cover onto the bed. When I got to Grandma's I thought she was still asleep, and I spent a few moments looking over some of my favorite pages in my Calculus notebook (such an interesting subject!). Then I went to wake Grandma, which accounts for why I spent so much time in her apartment. Well, when I went to wake her, Grandma's body was still warm—but her spirit had flown. It had happened, exactly what I'd been concerned about. Her wrinkled old face was crushed up against the plastic liner almost as if someone had held it there, and, as it had been a warm night and Grandma had asked me to turn off her air conditioner (despite the heat she was feeling chilly), either the sweat or something had formed that seal I'd mentioned and Grandma had suffocated. I just sat there and cried (remember how fond I am of my elders!), which is why I didn't phone 911 right away—I was too upset. Mother says not to let that worry me, Grandma had had a good long life and it must have been her time to go. She *was* still a bit warm when 911 did arrive a bit later, and the medic said there was a chance they could have revived her if they'd gotten there earlier—that she must have passed away only seconds before I arrived, or even during the time I was reviewing my Calculus notes.

Charlotte swore there'd been no plastic over on when she'd left, but it wasn't like anyone believed *her.* She said some pretty vicious things to me when we met by chance the next week, but I just ignored her. I knew she was acting out of guilt. Or, more likely, envy. After all, Grandma had died before she could change her will, so the money that would have gone to Charlotte went to Grandma's relatives—her sons and me (her only grandchild).

I believe Charlotte left town soon after—certainly she just seemed to disappear into thin air. I'm sure she simply picked up and moved—it wasn't as if anyone in town would hire *her* after what happened with Grandma. Anyway, as I said, this essay is dedicated to Grandma's memory, because it was her bequest to me that's enabled me to pay for college in the first place, especially nowadays when college is so costly (but worth it!), scholarships so limited, and just wardrobing oneself for college can be expensive as well. And of course, Mother and Father's earning power is not what it used to be, although their inheritance from Grandma, once they settle some ugly squabble with Uncle Leo, should be of major assistance. For the rest of my academic career, whenever I get a good grade (and I plan to get many!), I am going to dedicate it to Grandma's memory. And later, when I'm gainfully employed, I plan to make occasional donations to charity in Grandma's memory. I certainly expect to have an outstanding and lucrative career. I don't mean to boast, but I *already* have had an initial offer of employment made to me by a *very* important businessman, a Mr. Belliel. He approached me a while back, although for some reason I haven't heard from him lately.

Another of my guiding beliefs, in addition to the aforementioned beliefs in the importance of learning, of family, and of community, and one which I feel uniquely qualifies me for South Central, is in respect for one's elders. Of course I respected Grandma, but she was family. I also respect elders to whom I am not related. I even respected my third-grade teacher, Mrs. Manton, the one who retired from teaching to work in some library in New York City. Take for example my late Chemistry instructor, Miss Dale. She'd taught at Ridgefield High for ages and ages, and looked it too. Her small eyes were all watery and someone should have suggested she do something about the unsightly growth of hair on her upper lip—if it wasn't exactly a moustache, it certainly came close. Undersized yellow teeth and a slight stoop didn't add to her charms, but I for one would never dream of holding this against her, unlike some of my classmates. Eileen Kreckler said some of the *most* unkind things about Miss Dale in private to me, but I won't repeat them out of respect for the dead. And it's not as though that fat Eileen should have been criticizing *anyone's* appearance in the first place—people in glass houses shouldn't throw stones and all that. Anyway, I for one was always exceptionally kind to dear Miss Dale, no matter what Billy Spelling says he overheard. Billy spends too much time speeding around town on his motorcycle with that trashy Dolores Cadmus to be trustworthy. I am *much* cuter than Dolores could ever dream of being, plus she's only a junior. And I can't stand her sister either, that arty little Leah. Sometimes Billy doesn't even bother to wear a helmet. I think his brain must have windburn or something. I do hope he doesn't come to harm, ditto Dolores, due to some mechanical malfunction—motorcycles are notoriously unreliable, especially ones bought used, like I understand Billy's is.

At any rate, despite her appearance, I had volunteered to assist Miss Dale after school solely out of the goodness of my heart, *not* because, as Billy claims, I needed extra credit to pull my "C" average up to an "A." That's just ridiculous—I've never gotten a "C" in my life, and certainly wasn't about to get one in Chemistry. I would be able to prove this about my Chemistry grade if Miss Dale's grade book hadn't been incinerated. She never would have given me a "C"—Miss Dale and I were very close—no small feat when you consider that Miss Dale did seem to suffer from horrifying halitosis. I for one never said rude things about it behind her back, like when certain kids (who shall remain nameless) called her "Daletosis." Well, Miss Dale might have been getting on, but that made me respect her more for her decliningly successful attempts to contribute to our education. Nonetheless, I couldn't help but notice how forgetful Miss Dale was becoming; three times I observed her drive out of the teachers' parking lot by the entrance and twice she managed to lose the keys to the classroom even after she swore she'd left them right on her desk (of course she hadn't, but I didn't argue). Once her gradebook fell right off her desk into the trash can, but the janitor happened to see it sticking out from under some trash I'd put in when I was straightening up the room (which really needed it).

Being forgetful like that can make anyone cranky, and that must account for Billy Spelling's claim that he heard Miss Dale say the oddest things seemed to happen when I was around. *I* wouldn't trust a thing Billy Spelling says anyway, and I don't think anyone else does either, not since Miss Dale's pocketbook turned up in his knapsack! Well, I was so concerned about Miss Dale's forgetfulness that I spoke with Mr. Rutherwell, our school principal. He of course thanked me for my interest and said he'd speak with Miss Dale. However, when he did, she lied about *everything*—she claimed she'd never driven her car the wrong way or anything like that. She even made a few veiled accusations concerning the loss of her keys and the near loss of her grade book, or so Mr. Rutherwell reported to me later on. But I know he believed *me,* not that senile Miss Dale, because he laid his large hand on my shoulder and kept it there while we chatted, smiling down at me the whole time. I was wearing my new blouse that day, the one with the pretty ruffled neck that is *not* too low, no matter what Mother says. He told me a bright young girl like me should keep on keeping her eyes wide open and report back to him whenever I felt like it. As I mentioned to Mr. Rutherwell, after all Miss Dale had been teaching for ages and ages and that would get to anyone. Well, I'm sure Mr. Rutherwell regrets not acting decisively on what I'd told him.

It happened the following Thursday. As I mentioned before, I had volunteered to help out Miss Dale after school. This involved assisting Miss Dale conduct some experiments in the lab on four successive Thursdays. Well, I was assisting Miss Dale with these experiments, just mixing up chemicals in preparation for heating them on one of the Chemistry Lab's gas burners, when Miss Dale asked me to run to the Nurse's Office for a box of Kleenex and some aspirin (she had a dreadful cold which I was thankful I didn't get). It took me a while to find the nurse, because when I knocked on her door I knocked softly so as not to disturb someone inside who might be ill (even though it was after school, sometimes ill students linger until a parent picks them up) and I guess she didn't hear me. Since she didn't answer my knock, I presumed no one was there and went to look for her elsewhere before trying her office again a while later. So I was gone a good bit of time.

Apparently, in that time, Miss Dale had turned on the gas but had forgotten to light it right away, or so supposes the coroner. And of course, with that nasty cold she was suffering, she was unable to smell the accumulating gas. At any rate, I finally returned with the Kleenex and aspirin (though as Nurse Georgeson has made it her business to point out, she'd already given Miss Dale an entire bottle of aspirin and two boxes of Kleenex earlier that day—which *obviously* only goes to show how forgetful Miss Dale had become. I think Nurse Georgeson is just trying to make me feel guilty for being away from the lab for so long while the gas was building up. After all, if that nosy nurse had really been doing her job, she'd have sent Miss Dale home right after school for some much needed bed rest). At any rate, it was just as I was returning from my trip to the nurse, pausing on the way back to use the facilities, that Miss Dale evidently lit the match that ended up causing the explosion. My hand and wrist were singed painfully when I opened the lab door briefly to see if I could be of assistance (*after* I heard the explosion, that is), but I had to withdraw my arm immediately as the heat was too intense. Miss Dale never recovered consciousness and the entire lab needed major renovations afterwards. I am sorry to have to report that a few students (who again shall remain nameless, but I can tell you that one of them rides a motorcycle) were not entirely displeased about Miss Dale's untimely passing. You see, since her grade book had been incinerated in the explosion, there was no way of determining which student should receive which grades. Therefore, at my suggestion, Mr. Rutherwell made Chemistry that term a pass/fail class and passed us all. I received a commendation for attempting to save Miss Dale's life, which I thought of refusing, because after all, all I did was open the door for a second and sort of reach automatically into the room before I had to give up, but Mother and Father said I should accept it in Miss Dale's memory. So, to make them happy, I did just that. Thus, as you can see, my respect for my elders is so great I would risk anything—my life, even—if I thought my caring could be of some assistance.

So, in conclusion, I hope this essay will indicate why South Central University would be a better place for admitting me, Becky Sue Anderson. When I'm accepted, I plan to write a sweet little thank-you note to each and every member of South Central's Admissions Board, whose names and addresses I've taken the trouble to research. I do that because I care. It's like my dear Grandma said to me, "Becky Sue, if caring were a crime, they'd have to find you guilty!"

LETTERS
FROM
LEAH

FROM THE CORRESPONDENCE
OF LEAH CADMUS

The Alden Cottage
Westfleet, The Cape
Saturday, July 31st

Dear Anne-Marie,

I promised I'd write you a lot, so here goes. It's a pretty good start, too—we only got here last night. Mom rented the Alden Cottage sight unseen and for once she was lucky. Even Dolores is pleased and that takes some doing. Of course she nabbed the best bedroom. She says being seventeen she needs more privacy than I do, a mere babe of thirteen as she calls me. Then she added the remark that maybe *I* should have the better bedroom after all, since I needed more sleep. As usual I fell into her trap. "Why do I need more sleep?" I wanted to know. Dolores gave one of her smiles and said, "Beauty sleep, my child, that's what you need. If you sleep enough, at least you can dream you're beautiful." Of course she said it when Mom and Dad were out at the car starting to unpack, so she didn't get in trouble. And as you know, if I start to complain about something Dolores did when our parents weren't there, *I'm* the one who gets in trouble—they tell me not to be a tattletale and to learn how to stand up for myself. And if they catch Dolores in the act of being a pain, they usually think it's cute! I sure was unlucky when they handed out sisters. But at least next year Dolores will be a

senior—then it's college and she's out of my hair. No, not college—now Dolores says she's going to go to drama school. At any rate, despite all that crap about beauty sleep, Dolores snared the best bedroom (after Mom and Dad's, I mean), leaving me this tiny one.

But I don't care—I can still hear the sound of the breakers on the shore. I love that sound. Did I mention the house is right on a bluff overlooking the ocean beach? It's a long strip of yellow sand with the pounding surf on one side and steep dunes on the other. And the house is great, too—a little shingled cottage, a weather-beaten brown-gray in color with the sweetest green shutters. And it even has a backyard with a lovely garden, pretty rare for the Cape, I hear. The owners (I guess that would be the Aldens) must have hauled in a lot of good topsoil or something, because there's the prettiest bed of roses—lovely cream-colored ones, pale pink ones, and flaming red ones. They look beautiful against the background of the sea. And there's a quaint little brick path that leads all the way from the left side of our yard, through the middle of the rose bed, out the other side onto the grass, where it turns left and heads toward this wooden staircase built in the sand that goes down the dune to the beach where we swim when it isn't too rough and dangerous.

I couldn't figure out why the path would start on the left side of our yard, instead of at the house, but Dad guessed it probably used to run all the way along the bluff we're on, but the people next door took it out for some reason. The bluff is pretty high, so you have a sweeping view. Our cottage is one of twelve built along this narrow road, six on one side, six on the other. It's a dead-end road, so it's nice and quiet—very few cars. You'd love it here.

Well, that's it for now—Mom's calling me to come look at how pretty the sunset is and Dolores is screeching she can't find her lipstick. I'm going to run before Dolores shows up in my room, accusing me of stealing her lipstick! Besides, you know how much I love sunsets. They're so different every single night. I wish I could paint one!

I hope your job as a mother's helper isn't too gruesome!

Love,
Leah

The Alden Cottage
Sea View Terrace
Westfleet, The Cape
Tuesday, August 3rd

Dear Anne-Marie,

I meant to write you yesterday but it was such a beautiful beach day I just couldn't tear myself away from the water. We were on the bay beach where the swimming is best (Mom and Dad, Dolores and I) and we didn't get home until past six o'clock. I know that someone who wants to be a writer (if she's not a painter) should be able to write anywhere, but I need a desk and a chair or at least to be inside out of the bright sun. I'm on my way to getting a tan. And my hair already seems blonder—less mud-brown as Dolores calls it. If this keeps up I'm going to be kind of good-looking for a change, all beachy and California-like. Maybe when we start eighth grade next month, I'll get a boyfriend. You've already had two (three if you count David, which I know you try not to!), but I've never even been kissed. It's hard being the younger sister of the most popular girl at Ridgefield High, especially when she's such a cover-girl type—not that Dolores ever gives me any makeup hints (by the way, she found her lipstick in her makeup kit) or fashion advice except to tell me to stay in my room until being ugly comes into style.

Speaking of Dolores, her new thing is ghosts and other supernatural stuff. Weird, because as you know, I've always been fascinated by ghosts—it's been my dream to see one ever since I was little, but Dolores always teased me about it until now. At first I thought that for once Dolores was developing interests besides fashion, dating, and annoying me, but I was wrong. Two days ago I saw Dolores talking to this cute guy who works at The Pantry (the local food store that charges astronomical prices for the tourists but is much more convenient than the big supermarket over in Eastfleet). He looked like a college student and was just Dolores's type—kind of beefy with a big smile. "That's how it's done," Dolores said to me in an undertone on the way home, discreetly showing me his phone number on a scrap of paper so Mom and Dad couldn't see from the front seat. Dolores has always been lucky about meeting guys. In fact, she's just plain lucky in general—not like me. Anyway, today when we were in The Pantry I noticed Bob (that's his name, and he *is* in college, a sophomore at South Central University) was reading a book of true-life ghost stories—hence Dolores's newfound interest. She's nothing if not a quick study! Do you remember when she wanted to date that brain at Ridgefield High, the one in the Advanced Placement courses, just because his father was a Porsche dealer and he had one of those new roadsters before anyone else? (He's the poor fool she dropped like a hot potato, just to date Billy Spelling because she decided she liked his motorcycle more than a Porsche! Then he ended up dating that nasty Becky Sue Anderson!) When Dolores was trying to impress the Porsche guy she tried to bone up on molecular biology, his big interest. At first she thought it had to do with *moles!* Then she claimed she was joking about the mole part, just to get my goat. Maybe she was. It's hard to tell with Dolores. Sometimes I think she only acts dumb, sometimes I think it's the real thing. Sometimes I wish *I* were dumb, if it meant snaring a hunk like Bob. I know he's not my type, but he can't be a total jerk—after all, he does go to college. And Dolores says he even gets good grades. Of course, to Dolores that could mean straight C's! Anyway, all Dolores talks about now (besides Bob and how cute he is and how no boy will ever look at me twice) is ghosts. She's sure Westfleet must be haunted everywhere since it's such an old town (settled circa 1720—I looked it up) and used to have so many whaling vessels that were always capsizing and drowning all the poor sailors. "Of course," said Dolores, "I doubt *you'd* ever be able to see a ghost." "And why's that?" I asked (like an idiot). "Because," said Dolores, shaking her pretty hair that always falls just so and never looks bad, not even after she's driven in a convertible with the top down, "they'd take one look at you and be scared away!"

Why do I always fall into her stupid traps?

Anyway, I'm still having fun, even though it's a little lonely. I haven't seen any girls my age (or guys, either!) on our street. There was a block party and cookout last night and all there was besides Dolores and me were little kids and grown-ups. I wish you didn't have to be a stupid mother's helper and could have joined us—it really, truly is beautiful here.

I'm still waiting to hear from you (note the complete address at the beginning of the letter).

Love,
Leah

The Alden Cottage
Sea View Terrace
Westfleet, The Cape
Friday, August 6th

Dear Anne-Marie,

I've got big news—*big news!*

Do you remember Dolores's sudden enthusiasm for

ghosts? Well, it's kind of a coincidence, but maybe, just maybe, we've seen one. Yes, we. I saw it, too. So did Bob. (He's been up to the house a few times now, the first time being two days ago when I was out with Dad. Mom doesn't seem to mind, though I'm not sure she knows he's twenty.) Well, yesterday when Bob was over (timed for Mom and Dad's late afternoon walk on the beach), he said he was getting this weird tingly feeling. I asked if maybe he'd gotten too much sun (you should see his tan!), which made Dolores snicker.

"No, you cretin," she said. "Bob is kind of psychic. He tingles when he's feeling psychic."

"Actually," corrected Bob in his deep voice, "I'm not exactly a psychic. What I am is a sensitive."

I was thinking he didn't look too sensitive to me. I like sensitive guys, poet types (at least I would if I ever met one), and Bob is definitely no poet. According to Dolores he's majoring in phys ed.

"I bet you don't even know what a sensitive is," said Dolores in a superior voice. I didn't, but I didn't want to admit it. "You'd better clue the kid in," Dolores instructed Bob, acting as if she were a genius and I was some kind of half-wit. I couldn't believe Dolores knew what a sensitive was, unless Bob had just told her.

"Well," began Bob, checking the big gold waterproof watch he wears on his thick tanned wrist, "a sensitive is like someone who's really sensitive to what's called psychic phenomena. I'm not psychic myself, like I can't tell the future or anything, but I just kind of feel when there's psychic energy in the area."

"And do you feel it now, Bobby?" pressed Dolores, opening her brown eyes wide with wonder.

"Uh, yeah," Bob had to admit. "Really strong, too. Like in this very area."

"In the house?" cried Dolores, almost rubbing her hands together in anticipation. She started peering around excitedly, as if a ghost were going to jump out of the linen closet and start moaning.

"Uh, no," said Bob, shaking his head back and forth on his thick neck. "Uh, no, more like outside the house."

"On the beach?" asked Dolores, raising her prettily plucked eyebrows.

Bob kind of gave a shrug with his massive shoulders and made his narrow eyes narrower, as if he was thinking it over.

Dolores leapt from the wing chair she'd been curled up in like a cat and raced to the big window overlooking the yard and the ocean beyond. She stood and stared for a second, almost as if she were waiting for someone—or something. Then she gave a pretty little shriek, then a small gasp. Then she turned back toward the room, toward Bob and me, her mouth and eyes wide open with surprise.

"Oh, come on, Dolores," I said. "You can't fool me."

But for once Dolores didn't argue. She just turned back to the window and pointed.

Bob and I raced to her side.

Then we saw her, too.

It certainly looked like a ghost.

Remember I wrote you about this little brick pathway that runs across our yard? Well, this skinny little old lady was there, on the property to our left, right before where the path starts out of nowhere. At first she just stood there motionless. Then she lifted a thin arm and seemed to reach for something, making this movement like she was opening a gate—but, Anne-Marie, there wasn't any gate there, only empty air. Then she seemed to step through where a gate would be and walked slowly—*very* slowly—along the brick path, right in front of the window although she never looked over at the house, not even once. She was wearing only black, and her clothes looked hundreds of years old— I mean they were completely old-fashioned. She was even wearing these tiny lace-up black boots that went up to her ankles, the kind you see in old photographs. She was carrying this worn straw basket looped around her left arm. And she took such teeny tiny steps, almost as if she were floating above the ground and didn't want to disturb the air too much, if you know what I mean. Then, right in the middle of our yard, she paused—right where the brick path bisects the rose garden. She looked down at the roses as if she'd never seen roses before. Then she looked out to sea and seemed to tremble, just as though the wind were blowing through her. When she reached the point where the brick pathway turns and heads toward the stairs leading to the beach, she just kept on walking straight, footstep after tiny footstep, over the grass, always in a perfect line. Then, where our yard ends and the neighbors' begins, she paused again, again acting as if she were stopping at a gate. Once again she reached out her hand as if to open it. I swear she did—Dolores and Bob saw it, too, and you know Dolores isn't exactly the imaginative kind. Anyway, she withdrew her hand, and stepped gingerly over the invisible line between our property and the Kunkels' next door, and kept on walking. Bob called in a loud voice, "Hey, you!" But she didn't even flinch or peek in our direction. It was like she hadn't heard anything. It was so weird.

And another weird thing is, I know she doesn't live next door, either to the left (it's called Whitecrest Cottage) or the right (that's the Kunkel cottage), or anywhere else on Sea View Terrace for that matter. Remember we had that block party/cookout and we met all the families on the block, and no one had an old lady staying with them—and certainly not one dressed like she'd just strolled out of the 1800s! And why would someone walk across three private yards for no reason? It wasn't like she was taking a shortcut down to the beach.

Anyway, once she crossed over to the Kunkels' she really did seem to vanish from sight. We did look away, but only for a second—Dolores thought she'd seen something else approaching from the left. But the second we looked back, she wasn't there anymore. And I doubt she suddenly started running fast—she was really, *really* old. And her face—I'm going to try to draw it. It was amazingly pale, just as though she hadn't been out in the sun for ages and ages.

Her skin was so white you almost thought you could see through it. And she had the saddest expression—like she was thinking about some great sorrow that had happened centuries ago. And she truly did seem to float above the ground. Or maybe it was just the way she walked. It wasn't the way most people do—up and down a bit and from side to side. It was more like she was on wheels, if you can picture that.

After she'd vanished from sight, Dolores, Bob, and I just stood there in silence for at least fifteen seconds. Dolores was actually speechless, and you know how rare that is! Bob's handsome face almost looked a bit pale. He certainly had his mouth hanging open and all his straight white teeth were showing.

"Bob," said Dolores finally. "You were right. I think we've just seen a ghost!"

"Do you really think so?" I asked kind of faintly.

"Like duh," said Bob. "She didn't even turn around when I shouted."

"Didn't you see those old clothes?" added Dolores. "And didn't you see her stop to open those gates or doors that weren't there?"

"Ghosts do that kind of thing," Bob broke in. "I read it in my book."

"Of course they do," Dolores continued. "Certainly no normal, living person opens doors that aren't there."

My heart was pounding. I'd always wanted to see a ghost.

"Let's go outside and look around," said Dolores, racing toward the back door and outside to the yard. The next thing we knew, she was on her knees in the small patch of grass to the right of where the brick pathway turns. She was examining the grass intently, her back to us.

At last she turned around and faced us, Bob and me, where we stood watching by the back door. She had the strangest expression on her face.

"I can't believe it," she said. "There aren't any footprints in the grass!"

Bob and I ran over and checked. We even got down on our hands and knees. Dolores was right—there weren't any footprints. None. Of course I wondered if Dolores had pushed the grass back up, but I didn't think she had time. And why should she bother, anyway?

Next we ran to the edge of our property and looked to the right, across the Kunkels' yard. We could see three more cottages before the curve of the dune made it hard to see farther. And the little lady wasn't there—not in any of the backyards we could see. And she wasn't anywhere on the beach, either (unless she was hiding at the foot of the dune, which doesn't seem too likely). And there was no way she could have suddenly started walking fast enough to vanish from sight to cover three backyards to where we couldn't see anymore. No, she simply wasn't there anymore. She had disappeared.

"Maybe she turned off, into a house," I suggested.

"Maybe," said Dolores, "but that would be kind of odd."

"Why?" I wondered.

"Well," said Dolores, "we know she isn't staying anywhere on Sea View Terrace, right? If she were coming here on a visit, she'd walk on the road, wouldn't she? It's not like a little old lady—at least not a *living* little old lady!—to wander through backyards. I mean, ours is well kept, with the grass and the garden and the brick path and all, but look at the houses next to ours. Their yards are filled with beach grass and sand—and you know how hard it is to walk a long way on sand."

"And beach grass can cut you, too," added Bob, pointing to a few small cuts around his thick ankles. "They're from beach grass," he explained, as if we hadn't grasped the point.

"And the way she didn't even look up," said Dolores with a shudder. "It was like she didn't even see there were houses there—or didn't think the people in the houses would be able to see her!"

"Plus she didn't even seem to hear me when I called," put in Bob. "A real person would have reacted."

Mom and Dad thought we were making it up at first, when we told them about it at dinner. But as Dad pointed out, perhaps it was possible. After all, all our stories matched one another's—so at least we had all seen the same thing. And the lady's ignoring Bob's shouts was strange—not to mention her stopping to open gates that weren't there. Now that was *really* spooky! Mom was positive there was no old lady staying anywhere on Sea View Terrace.

"Everyone from Sea View Terrace was at the cookout," Mom confirmed. "And there was no old lady. And we haven't seen her on the beach or walking on the road, either."

"Maybe she lives nearby," suggested Dad.

"Does she, Bob?" asked Dolores. "You're from here, right? You know all the locals."

"Uh, no," said Bob, pausing to think. "I've never heard of her. But I can ask around at The Pantry tomorrow."

"It's a ghost," vowed Dolores, shaking her head to emphasize the point. "Bob even tingled. He's a sensitive."

Then followed a discussion of what it meant to be a sensitive and so on. Then came dinner and a moonlight swim. Now I'm sitting at the kitchen table, writing you. I'm so excited. What do you think? I'm almost entirely positive it was a ghost. As I said to Dolores, if I see it once more, I'll really be convinced. You can bet I'm going to be keeping my eyes open for it to show up again.

What a great summer! I've always wanted to see a ghost and now I have (at least I think I have). And Dolores can't tease me about it, because she's seen it, too. And she's even being a bit nicer than usual. This evening she said I was less painful to look at than usual (a big compliment, coming from her lipsticked little mouth!). Maybe just being near the ocean is bringing out the best in her. And I *do* look pretty good—I'm getting tanner by the day. All I need now to have a perfect summer is to be kissed . . . but that would be asking too much.

Oh well—I better stop. I hadn't realized how long this letter had gotten—but you know us budding writers!

Love,
Leah

Westfleet, The Cape
Monday, August 9th

Dear Anne-Marie,

More ghost news!

The day after I wrote you, I stopped by both our neighbors (to the left and right) and asked if they'd seen an old lady cross their property at five o'clock the evening before. The ones on the left had been out, so that was no help. The ones on the right had been at home, but busy getting dinner for their kids. Still, they were surprised to hear an old lady had crossed their property. "She must have been lost," the man guessed. But I know she wasn't—she didn't look lost. She was moving too steadily to be lost. Both neighbors were sure, too, there wasn't any old lady on the street, either renting a house or visiting one. They both just got here last week, and it's the first summer here for them, too, but still, if she was living somewhere in the area, you'd think one of them would have heard about her, wouldn't you?

I did all this investigating on my own. Dolores said she

was too embarrassed, and Bob was at work. I didn't tell the neighbors I thought it was a ghost. I might tell them later, and get a whole ghost watch going. Dolores thinks that's a good idea.

And Bob did remember to ask at The Pantry—and get this! He says no one there has heard of her, either! And a lot of people at The Pantry, like Bob's boss, have been living in Westfleet for generations.

And here's the icing on the cake. When Mom was at the supermarket over in Eastfleet, she started chatting with the checkout girl. The girl was from the area, and she was pretty sure she'd heard rumors from her grandmother that this bluff here is haunted! She didn't know anything else about it, though. But that's enough, don't you think?

We watched for her Saturday and Sunday nights, too, but no luck. Maybe she's a ghost who doesn't walk every night. I've just got to see her again! Maybe today will be the day. Bob said he was feeling kind of tingly, so that's a good sign.

Anyway, this is a short letter to make up for the last one. Thanks for yours, which came today. What a break about that handsome ninth-grader who lives next door! Some people have all the luck! And you even have a date planned! Write the second you have it and tell me everything! And I do mean everything!

Love,
Leah

Westfleet, The Cape
Tuesday, August 10th

Dear Anne-Marie,

Yes! It happened again! I am now an official ghost observer! And we even have proof—real, solid proof. Read on and you'll see what I mean.

It was last night. Bob had just gotten off work and had jogged up from The Pantry (it's around a quarter of a mile down the road). He and Dolores were sitting in the living room. They said they'd been chatting, but I didn't hear much conversation from my bedroom, where I was working my way through a book of short stories. Anyway, just before five o'clock, I heard Dolores give a little shriek, then she called in an urgent voice, "Leah—get in here quick!"

I raced to the living room, where I found Bob and Dolores standing stock-still at the window, staring off toward the left, toward where our property (and the little brick path) begins.

She was approaching slowly, carefully, little step after little step, still in the same ankle-length lace-up boots, still carrying the same small wicker basket. I got a better look at her this time, maybe because I was less astonished. Her skin is so white it looks like paper—very thin paper, the kind that's translucent. Her eyes were green and terribly sad. Maybe she's in black for a reason—like she's been in mourning through all these centuries. Anyway, after stopping to open the gate that's not there, she crossed the boundary from our neighbors' property into ours, taking those tiny steps, never once looking in our direction—up at the house. I mean, if you take a shortcut across someone else's property, you usually look up to see if there's anyone at home who might mind, right? Well, she didn't, she just kept on walking slowly, carefully, tiny step after tiny step, along the brick pathway. It was so spooky—just like last time she paused only once, right next to the white rosebush. She stopped and gazed down at a flower. Then she turned slightly, her back to us, and gazed out to sea. When she was looking out to sea she didn't move a muscle.

"I think I can see right through her!" cried Dolores in a breathless voice.

"Uh, me too, I think," put in Bob, his mouth hanging slightly open in wonderment.

I couldn't quite, but maybe it was the angle of the sun.

Then the ghost kept on walking, toward the right, to where the brick pathway ends, and onto the small section of grass. And once again, just like on Thursday, she stopped at the edge of our property and lifted up her right hand to open another invisible gate! And I'm not making it up or suffering from sunstroke, because Bob and Dolores saw exactly the same thing.

Bob and I were kind of tongue-tied with shock, but not

Dolores. At this moment she yanked up the screen and stuck her head out the window.

"Hey, you!" she shouted, even louder than Bob had the time before. "What are you doing here?"

The ghost didn't even look back or react in any way. She just passed through the invisible gate and kept on walking, as if nobody had called to her.

"Let's run after her!" bellowed Bob, almost flexing his muscles in anticipation of exercise.

"Do you think we should?" asked Dolores, uncharacteristically nervous.

"C'mon!" answered Bob, sprinting toward the screen door. Dolores and I followed in hot pursuit.

Out the door we barreled, down the three shallow steps and out into the backyard, all bathed in late-afternoon light. We veered over at an angle, to where the brick path ends and the grass starts. Dolores gave a cry and fell to her knees. At first I thought she'd fallen.

"Look at this!" she said in a hushed voice, pointing with a trembling finger toward something in the grass.

Bob threw his bulky form down next to her and so did I.

"Whoa!" said Bob, then gave a low whistle.

Dolores had picked something up from the grass, and handed it carefully to Bob. He examined it and passed it on to me.

Anne-Marie, you'll never believe me but I swear to God it's true.

It was a slip of paper, just a small slip, around four by six inches, but I think it's the most amazing thing I've ever seen (after the ghost and those photographs of you-know-who on the Internet!).

It was a small printed announcement, telling when the library was open and its hours. But it was more than that— *it was an announcement letting people know the library was open and ready for business.* I bet you're thinking, "So what?" Here comes the good part: The library in this town is way over one hundred years old—and this card was announcing *its original, first-time opening!* Now do you get it? No? Here's the clincher: *The printed notice was dated September 3rd, 1887!*

"Do you really think it's . . . um . . . um . . . this old?" asked Dolores, trying to do the math in her head but giving up.

Bob shrugged. "Dunno," he volunteered. "Maybe."

I examined it more closely.

"It's really good paper," I finally said, remembering stuff I'd learned in art class about printing. "Much better than what they usually use nowadays."

"How can you tell?" asked Dolores.

"The paper's really thick, for one thing. And you can tell it was hand-printed," I continued, glad for once to kind of show off some of the things I know. "Just look—see how black the ink is, and how you can feel where the type was sort of pressed into the paper."

Bob and Dolores examined the paper again. Dolores looked slightly interested and even Bob's square face showed a flicker of curiosity.

"You know," he said, "I just remembered something. The owner of The Pantry's son goes to some art school in Providence and I kind of think he's studying something about old printing or old books or something like that."

"Maybe you could show it to him!" cried Dolores, getting excited. "Maybe he could tell how old it is by looking at it!"

"Why not?" replied Bob. "It's worth a try."

At that point we remembered to look to see if we could spot where the ghost went after she'd left our property, but by then she had vanished. But at least we had this rectangular piece of paper she'd dropped—proof that she'd been there!

Mom and Dad had come back from a stroll on the beach by then (they didn't see her down there), and examined the paper. (I'd send you a Xerox but Bob took it with him to show to his boss's son). They agreed it was definitely an old-fashioned printing job on old-fashioned paper. The paper did look kind of old, too—it was a bit creased and frayed, especially around the edges. Still, I wasn't sure it looked like it was over a century old, but it's kind of hard to tell. Do you remember that old copy of *Little Women* my grandmother gave me, that her mother had, the one I was so proud of I brought it in for a book report back in third grade in Ridgefield Elementary? Remember I left it on the playground by mistake and that mean Mrs. Manton yelled at me for forty-five minutes? Well, it was printed in the 1870s (I think), but on such good paper it hardly looked old at all. So maybe it's the same with this paper. We're just lucky it landed in the grass in such a way a corner went into the earth so a sea wind didn't blow it away. Imagine losing the find of the century! Dolores said I should write to one of those TV shows or at least alert all the neighbors to keep a lookout for the next time the ghost walks. I wonder why she walks at five o'clock—I'd always thought ghosts walked at midnight or dawn, but maybe that's just the more famous ones.

I wish Bob hadn't taken the paper—I loved holding it, knowing a ghost had just dropped it. But it will be good to have an expert examine it.

Anyway, it's another long letter! I can't help it if I'm a budding writer. And artist, too. Besides a few sketches of the sea that just make it look like a flat blue-green puddle, the sketches I've been doing on this vacation have been pretty good. I did a really nice one of the cottage and some excellent portraits, if I say so myself. Dolores didn't like the one I did of her, but it looks exactly like her, especially the little sneer she gets around her mouth when she looks at me sometimes, the one hardly anyone else seems to notice (besides you!). I did a great one of Bob. You'll go ape over it. Dolores wanted me to give it to her, but I said that would depend on how she acted. I must say, she's still being kind of nice, not teasing me or tricking me or making me look like a total fool whenever she gets the chance. I think it's because we're all so into this ghost business, it doesn't leave her much time to be as nasty as usual.

I'm still waiting to hear about your date with Tad! And I'm still green with envy, at least from your description of him! Force your lazy self to put pen to paper and send me a full report! I mean it!

Love,
Your ghost-watching friend,
Leah

Westfleet, The Cape
Thursday, August 12th
(the month's almost half over!
Boo hoo!)

Dear Anne-Marie,

Finally—all the dirt on you and Tad. Your letter came yesterday and was so steamy I thought the glue on the envelope would come unstuck! (Just joking!) Your date sounds like fun. And have you seen him again? From what you said, it sounds like he's a pretty serious guy, not just a date-and-run kind of boy. Hope so, especially considering he's that cute (thanks for the further description!). Speaking of cute guys, guess what? (Isn't it dumb in letters when people ask questions like "guess what"? It's not like you're here in the room with me and could answer. But it's hard not to sometimes. Especially with you—we've been friends so long that when I write you, I almost feel you're here next to me, listening to my thoughts as I write them. Maybe I'm a "sensitive" like Bob says he is, not that he seems much like one to me.) Anyway—guess what? Can you guess? Well, here's a hint: Guess which formerly muddy-brown-haired but now blondish and tannish and kind of glamorous-in-my-new-bathing-suit girl was a little lucky for a change and sort of met someone?

It was yesterday. Mom and Dad and Dolores had gone to Eastfleet to the big supermarket to stock up on staples since it's so much cheaper there. I stayed home to keep an eye out for the ghost (whom we haven't seen since Monday), just in case she showed up at an odd time, not five like the last two times. And I was really ready for her. I was sitting outside on the back stoop, sort of wondering why she only seems to walk in one direction—we've never seen her walk back. In case being stared at might scare her off, I was pretending to concentrate on the book I was holding. Then somehow I forgot to pretend to concentrate and I was really doing it—I ended up getting pretty engrossed in my book. I forgot to look up every few minutes the way I'd meant to. Out of the blue I heard this exuberant whistling, sort of like an old folk song. It sounded familiar but I couldn't quite place it. At first I thought it was Bob, but I'd never heard him whistle. And somehow I didn't think he'd whistle like this, so sprightly and so musically. I imagine Bob whistling a marching song or the national anthem or something like that. So I looked up and there he was—the cutest boy I've ever seen and I mean it. I can't believe your Tad is half as handsome.

There he was, suddenly appearing out of nowhere at the top of the wooden stairs that go down to the beach. He was all suntanned and healthy-looking, like he spent half his time outdoors. He looked around seventeen or so. His hair was brown and shaggy and the wind kept blowing his long bangs across his forehead. I'm pretty sure his eyes were green. He had this great smile, like everything and everyone everywhere in the world was perfectly wonderful. He wore a light blue sun-bleached shirt that was unbuttoned and his chest was sort of muscular but still skinny. His jeans were rolled up at the ankles like he'd been wading in the water. It's weird—even though he looked so outdoorsy, he had such a poetic air to him, like when he wasn't running around in the sunlight, he'd be curled up reading poetry or just thinking deep thoughts.

I was so surprised to see him I have to admit I dropped my book (what a clod I can be, always at the worst moment, too). The noise seemed to startle him, because he looked over at me in surprise (he must have thought he was alone).

I summoned my courage and gave him a smile. And Anne-Marie, he smiled back, this glorious, happy smile, just as though no one had smiled at him for a long, long time (which I doubt!). Then he waved a brown hand in my direction and loped along the brick path toward the left. Right at the property line he looked once more in my direction, almost as if he didn't believe I'd still be watching him. Then he gave another huge smile and another wave. Then he gave this energetic leap, kind of like a pony or a tiger cub jumping simply for the pleasure of it, and so graceful, too! Bob could never be that graceful, not in a million years. He just leapt up in the air and came down a yard or so to the left, on our neighbors' property. Then he put his hands in his pockets, started whistling merrily to himself (he'd stopped when he saw me), and strode out of sight.

But he waved to me (twice!) and smiled at me (twice!). Now I'm kicking myself for not running after him or calling him over or doing something. What if he never comes back? What if he does? What'll I say? Help! Write back *immediately* and give me a good opening line. You're the expert around here (besides Dolores, but I don't want to tell her, she'd just tease me).

So you can bet I'll be sticking close to the house, boy-watching and ghost-watching. I don't know which I want to see more! I think it's a tie. No, maybe not. I'd go for the boy!

Write soon! Telegram! Give me that opening line that will make him stop in his tracks and want to talk to me!

Love,

Your boy-watching friend,

Leah

·　　·　　·

Westfleet, The Cape

Friday, August 13th

Dear Anne-Marie,

Just a quick note, good news and bad.

The good news: I saw the ghost again! This must make me an official ghost-watcher. She showed up last night, at almost exactly five o'clock again, walking from left to right (again), still wearing black, still carrying her empty basket. This time I noticed she wore a small silver locket on a chain around her neck. Once again she paused on the left as if to open an invisible gate, walked along the brick path, stopped by the rosebush, looked out to sea, then kept on walking, pausing again to open another imaginary gate, then left our property. And I was brave, too, just like Dolores. She was halfway across our yard when I called out to her, "Hello! Hello! Can I help you?" She totally ignored me, just keeping on walking as I shouted, almost as if the sound of my voice was going straight through her, if you know what I mean. I felt so spooked out by this—it made me *really* believe she's a ghost. I mean, I believed it before, but now I *really* believe it, as though it has finally sunk in all the way. It gave me the chills—here was a spirit, walking across my yard, and I was all alone with her (Mom and Dad were having a cocktail with some neighbors, and Dolores was hanging out at The Pantry with Bob). I was going to follow her, but I got too nervous to do it all by myself. What if she was an evil spirit and led me somewhere really spooky, like a graveyard? Not that she looks mean or anything—I looked at her extra carefully this time and she definitely looks more thoughtful and wistful and faraway than evil, that's for sure. Once she passed out of sight I felt braver, and stepped out into the yard to see if I could spot where she went after our yard—and I couldn't see her anywhere! So I rushed inside and did a pretty decent drawing of her from memory. It looks like her, at least I think it does.

The bad news: Dreamboat hasn't shown up again, and my casual questions to my neighbors have revealed no one who knows him or has seen him. I bet they're starting to think I'm kind of nosy (or weird!), always asking questions about different people no one else seems to have seen!

That's it for now—if I stop here I can get this down to The Pantry, where the mailbox is, in time for tonight's pickup.

I'm still waiting for your handy list of opening lines! Hurry!

Love,
Leah

P.S. Forget tonight's pickup—big news! Bob just showed up with Dolores and guess what? (Sorry, there I go again!) He showed the paper to his boss's son, the one who goes to RISD (that's Rhode Island School of Design to those in the know), and he says there's no doubt about it—that slip of paper Dolores found *is* over a century old! There's something about the weave—Bob couldn't remember the details. The boss's son was so impressed he brought it to his professor, who not only agreed with him but is bringing it to some meeting of experts they're having later in the month (but he promised to return it afterwards). So we have proof! If that cute guy comes back, I figure I can tell him all about it. I mean, who could be more fascinating than a girl who's seen a ghost up close and even has evidence to prove it! He'll just have to stop walking and chat! I only hope I'm brave enough to start the conversation! Wish me luck!

Westfleet, The Cape
Sunday, August 15th

Dear Anne-Marie,

Only ten more days and our four weeks are up, and I haven't seen the ghost or the guy since I wrote you last. Yes, I know that was only two days ago, but waiting's not easy! By the way, I'm still waiting for your list of impressive opening lines, just in case mine about seeing a ghost doesn't work.

Dolores had a good idea for once. She said I should make up a flyer about the ghost, get copies made, and put one under the door of all twelve houses on Sea View

Terrace, telling about the ghost sighting and requesting everyone to keep their eyes open. We could even include a copy of my drawing (luckily it's in black and white, so it will reproduce easily). Dolores said she would sign it with me, and Bob (who showed up in this skimpy Speedo) said he would, too. He even volunteered to copy it for free (with some prodding from Dolores—and I can't believe how nice she's being) on the Xerox machine they have at The Pantry. Mom and Dad said weren't we going a bit overboard with this ghost business, maybe it was just some weird old lady, etc. Of course I reminded them that Bob, who's from Westfleet, had asked all the old-timers he knew, and not one had ever heard of anyone staying in or visiting Westfleet who resembled our ghost—not to mention that library announcement and the rumor Mom heard at the supermarket about our bluff being haunted. Dad said that was all well and good, but wasn't there usually some logical explanation for psychic phenomena? You know my Dad, always practical! Anyway, I got busy and here's what I came up with (with a little advice from Bob and Dolores):

ATTENTION NEIGHBORS ON SEA VIEW TERRACE:

Ghost Sighting!!!

Yes, a ghost has been sighted three times near Sea View Terrace, crossing the backyard at the Alden Cottage (18 Sea View Terrace), heading from Whitecrest Cottage (16 Sea View Terrace) toward the Kunkel cottage (20 Sea View Terrace), where she vanishes!

Keep your eyes open for her, and please report all sightings or other information to us in 18 Sea View Terrace! Thank you very much!!!

A sketch of the ghost:
[Here's where I'll put a copy of my drawing]

PLEASE CONTACT:

Leah Cadmus
Dolores Cadmus
(18 Sea View Terrace)
Bob Miner
(c/o The Pantry)

Bob took it and my drawing and is going to Xerox it. Tonight I'm going to put a copy under all the doors on Sea View Terrace, or at least I will whenever Bob brings them back (he might have to work late tonight). I'd go pick them up, but I want to be home at five o'clock in case the ghost walks. (She really does seem only to walk at five o'clock. I wonder why.) Plus, I hate to leave home at all in case *he* shows up! Mom can't understand why I've lost interest in going with them to the bay beach and suddenly prefer the ocean! I've been aching to tell someone, so I'm glad I've got you to confide in. I was almost tempted to tell Dolores, since she's been acting so nice lately, but you know how nasty she can get about personal stuff. In fact, I think you're the only one who really sees through Dolores's act—not even my parents do.

I'll stop now so I can give this to Mom to mail on her way to the beach,

Love,
Your watchful friend,
Leah

P.S. I almost forgot. Say hi to Tad. Tell him he's a lucky guy to have had three dates with date-'em-and-dump-'em Anne-Marie! (Just kidding!)

Westfleet, The Cape
Tuesday, August 17th

Dear Anne-Marie,

I know I just wrote you Sunday, but I wanted to tell you that we saw the ghost again last night—all of us (Mom and Dad, Bob, Dolores, me). Exactly at five she appeared, just like all the times before. (I realized she always walks on Mondays and Thursdays—hmm, there's got to be some mystical reason.) We all saw her pause at the border of Whitecrest Cottage on our left, open the nonexistent gate, walk a bit, pause by the roses, look out to sea, then walk toward the Kunkels', pause, open the second nonexistent gate, then keep on going. We all hollered, even Dad, who has a pretty loud voice (and suddenly seemed to have become a believer!), but the ghost didn't pause or look around or anything—she just kept on walking. I wanted to go after her (I was feeling braver) and so did Dad, but Bob grabbed me (he's pretty strong!) and held me back.

"Don't!" he said in a severe voice that made even Dad stop in his tracks. I thought perhaps he was scared, but it turned out that he'd done some reading in his book on ghosts, and somewhere in it, it said you shouldn't disturb a ghost in the middle of its habitual walk. He forgot why you shouldn't—something about it causing the ghost further unhappiness (ghosts only walk because they're unhappy, it seems). Bob promised to lend me the book once he's finished it.

I ran for my camera (after I'd tried to run after the ghost), but Dolores had finished off my roll of film without telling me, taking pictures of Bob. Damn her! She at least could have told me, or bought a new roll to replace the one she used up. But not Dolores! I wish I'd thought of trying to take a photograph of the ghost a bit earlier. Maybe next time.

But I can't be too mad at Dolores—she and Bob distributed the flyers at every house on Sea View Terrace all by themselves as a favor to me. Bob only printed up exactly enough, so I don't have any extra in case I want to give one to my mystery boy if conversation fails me. Or to send one to you—but at least you saw my plan for it, so you know what's in it.

Oh—thanks for your list of opening lines. I can't believe they work! I think I'll stick with my idea of talking about ghosts!

Love,
Leah

Thursday, August 19th

Hello again—

Yes, it's me. It's Thursday, so I'm waiting for the ghost. Everyone else is at the bay but I'm here—you know why. I've got some time to kill so I thought I'd write you. Sorry if that sounds insulting, but you know I don't mean it like *that!*

I just got back from running an errand at The Pantry. It was kind of weird—I saw some of our neighbors from Sea View Terrace. I thought they'd ask me more about my flyer, but no one did. Some looked sort of amused while others seemed to give me dirty looks! Maybe they don't believe in ghosts—well, it's not my fault if they're doubters. Wait till they see the old ghost lady for themselves! They'll have to change their tune then! Bob had to do something in the storeroom when I was there, so we didn't have a chance to speak. I could hear him laughing his loud low laugh as they moved around merchandise. I did stop the owner of

The Pantry, Bob's boss, and asked him if his son was around—I wanted to ask him about the paper and the printing on the announcement the ghost dropped. It was weird—I guess there must be two owners of The Pantry. The one I spoke with (and I know he's the boss because he's always there, chatting happily with people who buy a lot and glaring at any employee who doesn't look busy enough), well, I asked him if his son was around and he said, "What are you talking about—I've got three daughters! Three too many in my opinion," he added as a joke. So I guess there's another owner I don't know about. I was going to ask but I got too embarrassed.

Anyway, now it's quarter to six and no ghost. I sat quietly so as not to disturb the ghost on its walk, the way Bob's book says you're supposed to, but she never appeared. She always walked on Thursdays before. What if we scared her away by yelling at her? Ghosts might be pretty sensitive.

Here comes my family—gotta go.

Love,
Leah

Friday, August 20th

Dear Anne-Marie,

I'm so mad I don't know what to do! That's why I'm writing. It's Dolores. I knew her being nice would never last. I was walking down Sea View Terrace, keeping my eyes open for both the ghost and the guy, when I happened to stop at the trash can outside the Kunkel cottage to throw out a gum wrapper. Guess what I found in the trash? My flyer. But that's not the bad part. I looked closer at it—remember, Bob only printed enough to distribute, no extra, not even for me. Now I see why. Guess what Dolores and Bob did before they Xeroxed it? They whited out their names so only mine appeared! Now everyone thinks *I'm* the only one who saw the ghost and my own family didn't! I hate Dolores! Can you believe it? And Bob. He might not be a rocket scientist, but I thought at least he was a decent guy. Dolores must have talked him into it. Well, when they interview me for a big TV report about ghosts and psychic phenomena I'll have the last laugh.

Your angry friend,
Leah

Sunday, August 22nd

Dear Anne-Marie,

You're not going to believe what happened. This has been the—I don't even know what—just the most, *most* day I ever had. You'll see what I mean.

I was alone again—Mom and Dad and Dolores were at the beach and Bob was at work I guess. I'm not talking to

Dolores anymore anyway, so I don't even care where she parks her bikinied little body just as long as I don't have to look at it. "I didn't think you'd mind so much, having only your name on the flyer," she said with a straight face. "You're the one who's the most interested anyway."

So there I was, sitting on the back stoop. I was trying to sketch the ocean and was still ending up with something that looked like a flat green puddle. I was about to give up and throw my pad in the trash when I had a new idea about how to draw the ocean—kind of to start with my feelings and then try to make it look real. I'm not sure I'm explaining it well, but somehow it worked. I really truly made a drawing (I was using pastels) that looked like the ocean— wild and beautiful, strong and subtle, filled with changing colors but never really changing at all. I got so involved with my drawing I forgot to watch for the ghost or the guy. Then I felt something brush against my shoulder, like a gentle wind. It made me shiver—but deliciously. I looked around and there he was—right next to me! I hadn't heard him approach. And, Anne-Marie, he was so beautiful I thought I'd faint! His eyes *are* green, like the sea, and his thick brown hair has auburn streaks in it from being outside. His skin was glowing with health and his eyes glowing with humor and liveliness and interest. He was still wearing the same clothes as when I saw him before—the shirt open, the pants rolled up a bit. He was barefoot, which I hadn't noticed before.

"Very pretty," he said, surveying my picture.

I blushed and thought, "Thank You, God—he started the conversation, not me!"

"Thanks," I said (clever response, eh?). "I'm Leah."

"I'm Willy," he said, smiling so his white teeth showed and these adorable dimples appeared in his cheeks. He kept his hands thrust in his pockets, which gave him kind of a boyish look.

Then he sat down with a sudden move, right in front of me, there on the grass at my feet, and examined me with lively interest.

"You must be an unusual girl," he said after a few moments' examination.

"Thank you," I said (it was a compliment, wasn't it?). "I guess I am."

"You are," he said, taking his left hand out of his pocket and brushing his bangs out of his eyes. "I know you are. I can tell."

I smiled. He had this beautiful voice, kind of like the sea, though I really don't know what I mean by that. But I heard the waves on the shore in the background, and the wind through the scrub pines and the beach grass, and somehow his voice fit in with all that, but not that it was whistly or anything, it was low and strong.

I forgot all about my plan to start the conversation by talking about ghosts. I guess I was too excited to think straight. Or maybe I got a better idea.

"Would you . . . Would you . . . I mean, I'd like to draw a picture of you. Would you mind?"

Willy gave another smile and looked amused—but pleased, too.

"No one's given me a second glance for a long time," he said, but without sounding like he was fishing for a compliment.

"That can't be true," I said, and flipped the page in my pad and started drawing. It was like heaven—I got to stare at the most beautiful guy I've ever seen, and there he sat, smiling back at me. He seemed rather shy, like he wasn't used to conversation much.

So, as I sketched, I remembered my idea to talk about the ghost.

I had just started telling him about her when he laughed so hard he almost fell over.

"What's so funny?" I asked—but I didn't mind him laughing at me. It wasn't like when Dolores laughs at me, because when Willy did he laughed so merrily and seemed so nice about it. He was just happy, I can't explain it any other way.

"That's no ghost," he finally said when his laughter had subsided.

"But—" I tried, but he kept on.

"No, you silly, that's just Sis—Sis Blakley. She only looks a bit like a ghost, I guess. She's—let's see—she's eighty-seven. The Blakley family has lived around here for ages and ages. She's the last. In fact, they used to own all this land on the bluff here, overlooking the ocean, way before there were houses on it."

"But where does she live?" I asked as I sketched. And it was so weird. I didn't care for the moment about not having seen a ghost—I was spending time with Willy.

"If you go to the end of your street—Ocean View, whatever you call it—you'll see this area of scrub pines, like a small forest."

"I've seen it," I said, "but don't tell me she lives in a forest."

Willy gave another of his smiles.

"Course not. But there's a little path that leads into the forest, goes a way, and near the middle is an old cottage over a century old. That's where Sis Blakley lives."

"But there must be another way in."

"Certainly—there's a narrow drive that opens up off the main road and goes off at an angle. But the sign reading her name fell down decades ago and I suppose she never bothered to put it up again. She's rather a recluse, you see—she likes being alone. Or at least she's just used to it, it's hard to tell. I myself check in on her from time to time, to make sure she's all right."

"But her clothes—"

"She wears the same clothes she's always worn," explained Willy with a shrug. "Some people are like that."

"But we called and called," I said as my hand flew over the paper, almost by magic, capturing Willy perfectly—his wildness and his sweetness, his sense of humor and his air of mystery.

He smiled again. "Deaf," he explained. "It happened when she was around, oh, sixteen. An infection, I seem to recall. She has one of those hearing things, but I imagine she doesn't like wearing it."

"But she stopped and seemed to open gates," I persisted. "It was weird."

"Not really. You see, this once was Blakley land. Where your cottage is, the yard part I mean, was actually where, ah, Sis's mother had a rose garden. The garden used to be bigger—the size of this entire yard. But at least when they built this cottage they kept part of the garden. It's good, you know, to keep old things."

"I know," I said, still drawing. "I like things from long ago."

"I can tell," said Willy, looking at me so hard I felt it and looked up from my drawing. I found him staring thoughtfully at me. "Well," he continued, "back to your question about the gates. There used to be more wildlife back when Sis Blakley was a girl, back when this was the Blakleys' garden. There were deer and rabbits, so the Blakleys put up this picket fence all around the garden. It was up from when Sis was a little girl until the land was sold. So I guess she reaches for the gates from force of habit."

"And the brick path was there then, too?"

Willy nodded. "It ran all along the bluff. But only part of it remains, the part on this property."

"But why did no one know her?"

"Remember she's a recluse. Only old families know her, people who've lived here awhile. She only goes out twice a week these days."

"But someone from an old family didn't know her," I said, thinking of Bob. "He even asked other people from old families."

"That I can't explain."

"But she just seemed to disappear," I tried again, not because I still believed she was a ghost, but because I wanted to get all the facts straight.

Willy smiled again. "Perhaps you didn't look carefully enough. You see, the Blakley property ended just beyond the house to your right. In the old days, Sis would walk to the market and she always tried to stay as much as possible on Blakley land. So, again by force of habit, she would walk this way, along the bluff, jutting back to the road after the house next door. There used to be a footpath there, back in the old days."

"But where is she going now?" I wondered.

"To the market still."

I was silent for a second. Then I remembered the library announcement.

Willy shrugged and his open shirt flapped in the sea breeze. "Perhaps it was something she'd found at home and was taking to show someone, then lost," he suggested.

I was silent again as I drew and thought.

"So I didn't see a ghost at all," I said slowly. "Only an old lady, living in the past."

Willy smiled once more, this time more of an enigmatic smile.

"Sis Blakley always was a rare one," he said, suddenly jumping to his feet and stretching. He stretched like a cat, with total pleasure and total abandon, throwing his long arms in the air and reaching out like he was trying to touch the sky.

"Let me see," he said, now standing next to me where I sat, looking down at my drawing.

I got to my feet and showed him the drawing. He examined it gravely, looking at it with a knowing, observant expression. Then he smiled, but it was less the happy smile I'd captured in the portrait and more of a serious smile.

"It looks just like me," he said finally. "I am glad," he went on, "to be so well remembered."

Then he looked right at me. Our eyes met and he looked down, deep into mine, and I looked into his. All I could see was that beautiful green. It was like looking into deep water, down far into the sea. Then the moment passed and he gave the widest smile.

"Thank you," he said.

Then he leaned forward and kissed me, right on the lips. Oh, Anne-Marie, it was so sweet and wonderful that I can barely start to really describe it. It was like a cool wind on a warm day, like diving in deep water, like a song, like everything wonderful. It felt so wonderful I'm not even sure I felt it at all.

Then he was gone—he turned around and headed across

the lawn, toward the wooden stairs. I blinked and he had already vanished. I guess he took the stairs in a great leap. I would have run to the top of the stairs to wave good-bye or yell my address after him or somehow ask him more about himself, but I felt paralyzed. My lips were still tingling and my heart was thumping like it had gone crazy.

I had been kissed. Me. Leah Cadmus. Unlucky Leah. Not so unlucky Leah.

I don't know how long I just stood there—it might have been minutes or hours or days. (I know it wasn't days, obviously, but it could have been!)

My happy state was interrupted by Dolores.

"Still ghost-hunting?" she snickered. I suddenly figured out that she had known all along there wasn't a ghost, that once again I'd fallen into one of her traps. I knew it, I just knew it.

At first I felt so angry I thought I would explode. I could feel this seething anger, this fury, rising up through me like lava in a volcano—I could almost feel it burning me inside as it rose. I could even almost see it, as weird as that might sound. I thought that once all this lava, this rage, rose all the way to the top that I would start screaming at dumb Dolores and start shaking her until that smug smile fell off her lipsticked little mouth. I really thought that. But then, when my anger reached the top of me, just when I thought I'd really explode like a volcano, it simply vanished—like mist in the morning, like water in the sand, like a wave back into the sea. It wasn't like I'd decided not to get angry, or was sitting on my anger, it just went, like a strong wind had blown out a tiny flame. Willy's kiss made everything different, everything better.

"There's no ghost," I said simply. "I just heard."

Dolores's face fell. I couldn't tell if she was more disappointed that I'd found out the truth or that I wasn't going to give her the satisfaction of acting all upset, the way I usually do.

"Darn!" she said. "Bob and I were having such a good time yanking your chain all around Westfleet. God, were you a sucker!" she added, looking hopeful that I'd yell or cry or something.

"What's this?" asked Mom, coming up behind us. "Did someone see the ghost again?"

"There's no ghost," I repeated simply.

"It was a gag," explained Dolores, acting like the whole thing was pretty funny. "Bob and I were just joking around."

"But—" started Mom, looking confused.

"It's only this eccentric old lady named Blakey or something who's lived alone in some shack in the woods ever since she was a girl because of some family tragedy or something sappy like that. She's as deaf as a post," continued Dolores, "and forgets her family doesn't own this land anymore. Twice a week she walks to the store and Bob's boss drives her back when she's filled her little straw basket."

"But I thought Bob said no one knew—" Mom was pointing out when Dolores interrupted.

"We were just teasing Leah," explained Dolores. "It's not my fault she's so gullible. Anybody who's lived in Westfleet more than a month knows about this old dame."

"But didn't someone say she left no footprints—" Mom tried again.

"I roughed up the grass before Leah got there."

"Really, Dolores!" said Mom, not even getting mad. "You've got to go easy with these practical jokes!"

"Right, Mom."

I could feel Mom looking at me—waiting, I guess, for me to react or something. But I didn't, I just stood there, still feeling Willy's kiss on my lips—a feeling that was bigger than my anger at Dolores, bigger than anything.

"But what about that library thing," asked Mom, "the one the boss's son said was so old? The one Leah examined?"

Dolores almost swelled with pride. "First of all, Bob's boss doesn't even have a son. And that announcement was a facsimile of the original announcement. They found a bunch of old paper somewhere and printed up a lot for the library's centennial a few years back. Bob happened to have saved one. It was almost an exact copy of the original."

"What was a copy?" asked Dad, who'd just appeared.

Once the whole thing had been explained, he gave a low chuckle and said, "Good one, Dolores! You sure pulled the wool over all our eyes!"

Then he smiled and so did Mom.

Mom and Dad moved off, never even remarking on how

nasty Dolores and Bob had been to me with this ghost business. I'll never know why they don't notice how nasty Dolores is, but like I've been saying, this time I just didn't care. Maybe I would never care again. Even her gloating expression didn't get to me.

"What's gotten into you?" asked Dolores, staring hard at me, her expression changing to one of real disappointment. "Usually you'd be whining and weeping about how unfair I am. What is it?"

I smiled. I could still feel the memory of Willy's kiss on my lips. And I had his portrait to look at. I didn't care about Dolores anymore. She'd lost her power over me.

"What is it?" repeated Dolores irritably.

I kept on smiling, thinking about Willy.

I even smiled at Dolores, before wandering off to look at my drawing again.

"What is it—what is it?" yelped Dolores as I walked off, even stamping her foot in annoyance. It was the first time *I* had made *her* angry, the first time *I* had power over *her.*

"What is it?" she repeated, sounding angrier or more frustrated.

I didn't even bother answering.

Willy—I was thinking about Willy.

Love,
Leah

•   •   •

Westfleet, The Cape
Tuesday, August 24th

Dear Anne-Marie,

I know I could tell you all this when I see you in a few days, but I feel like writing it down, kind of to sort it out. We leave tomorrow.

Yesterday, Mom managed to tell Dolores to apologize to me. Then, if you can believe it, Mom told me *I* had to apologize to Miss Blakley. It seems she'd spotted one of my flyers and of course recognized herself on it! I guess she wasn't too pleased—supposedly that's why she stopped walking across our property on her twice-a-week stroll to The Pantry. I imagine no one likes someone spreading rumors they're a ghost! I don't know why Dolores didn't have to apologize, too, but she didn't.

So I walked along the main road until I spotted this weedy, rutty dirt road that led through an overgrown scrubby pine wood. A little stick stood by the road that must once have held a name on the top.

I followed the road as it curved its way through the pines, around a bend, and down into a hollow where the house was nestled like a bird in a nest. No wonder it's not visible from the road! It was a small shingled house, very old. I'd learned the Blakleys had built it in the 1800s and that old Miss Blakley had been born in this very house. It was hard to imagine someone so old and ghostlike ever being a newborn baby.

I was praying she wouldn't yell at me and call me an idiot for spreading the word around Westfleet that she was a ghost. I should have known Dolores was setting up one of her traps by how nice she was acting. And of course she talked Bob into it—she always wraps her boyfriends around her little finger.

A riot of blue morning glories was massing its way up and around a shaky trellis next to the front door. You could tell the door had once been painted blue to match the morning glories, but now the paint was peeling and flaking and the door almost looked like a piece of driftwood, it was so stripped bare by the elements.

There wasn't a doorbell, so I used a tarnished knocker.

Then I waited.

I was just telling myself I was in luck, that Miss Blakley was out or fast asleep somewhere or too deaf to hear the knocker, when tiny slow footsteps sounded inside, gradually nearing the door.

The door opened. I was face-to-face with Miss Blakley. Her skin was even whiter and more ghostlike close-up, yet surprisingly unwrinkled. Her white hair had traces of yellow and instead of being worn up in a bun (the way I'd always seen it), now it was hanging way down her back in long waves. She was small and skinny and looked a bit fragile. I noticed she was wearing a hearing aid—she hadn't been when we'd seen her out walking. Her eyes were alert and examined me with interest. She didn't look exactly pleased.

"So," she said, not wasting any time, "might I presume that you are the young girl with the overactive imagination?"

I blushed and started feeling like a total idiot. It might have been better if she'd just yelled at me instead of speaking in a normal tone. Sometimes it's worse when people act nice.

"I'm sorry," I finally said, trying to unblush my face.

"No harm done, I suppose," replied Miss Blakley after a pause. "Although it had never occurred to me I bore any resemblance to a ghost."

My blush got blushier, if that's a word. I was wishing she would just thank me for apologizing so I could leave. After all, it was my last day and I was hoping to get home and see Willy one more time. I certainly didn't want to see anyone else in Westfleet, not with my new reputation as the girl who cried ghost!

"Do you really think I resemble a ghost?" persisted Miss Blakley.

"I guess I really don't know what a ghost looks like."

"Evidently," said Miss Blakley, raising an eyebrow and looking somewhat superior.

"Um, I, um, have something for you. To show I'm sorry," I told her, pulling out my sketchbook.

Miss Blakley looked somewhat weary at the thought of receiving a gift. She heaved a small sigh and said, "Yes?"

I tried to hurry and at last found the drawing of Miss Blakley I had done from memory. It really was a good likeness. My dad had suggested I give it to her as a peace offering.

I ripped it out of the pad it was in, and soon Miss Blakley was holding her portrait in her white hands.

"Surprisingly proficient," she at last said, after examining the portrait with care. "I shall keep it," she added in a slightly softer voice.

I gave a little smile. So did Miss Blakley.

"Thank you for such a pretty apology," said Miss Blakley, nodding her old head to indicate the interview was at an end.

I was turning to go when I remembered something.

"Oh," I said. "I wrote your name on the back. In calligraphy."

Miss Blakley turned the thick paper over to where I'd written in pretty blue letters, "To Sis Blakley with apologies from Leah Cadmus."

Miss Blakley stared at the writing and started shaking. I hadn't thought it was possible, but she turned even whiter. Her hand trembled so much she dropped the portrait, which flew out at zigzag angles the way paper can, out onto the front walkway, landing near the morning glories.

I ran to get it, returning with it in my hand and, I suppose, a worried look on my face. I was thinking that Miss Blakley must be feeling tired all of a sudden. But when I held out the portrait for her to take back, she grabbed my shoulders instead and squeezed firmly.

"Who told you my name?" she demanded in a quavering voice.

"They—they all know it," I replied, thinking she must be such a recluse she didn't think people even knew her name anymore. "My sister's friend lives around here and he said the Blakley family—"

"Not my surname," interrupted Miss Blakley, clutching my shoulders so tightly they were starting to hurt. "Not my surname," she repeated. "My nickname. Sis," she added slowly, as if just saying the name was painful.

"It was—" I started, but Miss Blakley kept on talking, almost as if she were talking in her sleep.

"No one has called me that for seventy years," she said, her voice sounding all faraway and misty. "And even then only one person ever called me that. Not even my parents—to them I was Wilhelmina."

She pinched my shoulders more tightly and stared at me. I couldn't tell if she was angry or scared or what. But she certainly stared hard.

"I'm sorry," I mumbled. "I didn't know it was a private nickname. I just thought it—"

"Who told you?" demanded Miss Blakley, her voice now a whisper.

"Willy."

"Willy," repeated Miss Blakley hoarsely. "Willy."

"That's right," I said. "You know each other, right?"

"Know each other?" repeated Miss Blakley, staring hard at me. "Know each other?" she said again, as I wished to myself Willy had told me it was such a private nickname. "Of course we know each other."

Miss Blakley let go of my shoulders and started fumbling with the locket she wore around her neck. At last she got it open. She held it up to my face, but she was trembling so much I couldn't see what was in it.

I put my sketch pad and the portrait of Miss Blakley down on the ground and, very gently, eased the open locket from between Miss Blakley's fingers and held it steady. It was silver and oval-shaped; each of the open halves contained a tiny portrait. On the left was a young girl, around eight years old, with green eyes, long blond hair, and a serious expression. It took a few seconds, but I recognized Miss Blakley, back when she was a child. Then I looked at the second portrait. At first it didn't make sense—no sense at all. None. It was done at the same time as the first, I could tell by the style. It was of a boy, also with green eyes and a serious expression, a boy who resembled Miss Blakley, a boy I thought I recognized. I guess my face showed my utter confusion.

Miss Blakley took back the locket, closed it, and let it fall on her breast.

Then, very gently this time, she laid her hands on my shoulders.

"Of course I know Willy," she said in a breaking voice. "He is the only one who ever called me Sis. Willy is my brother."

"Willy is your brother?" I barely managed to say.

Miss Blakley gave a sad smile and looked at me more kindly, even though I saw tears forming in her green eyes.

"Willy Blakley drowned seventy summers ago, in the high surf, right in front of where the new cottages now stand. My parents sold the land a while after his death, although I walk there still, looking out to sea where last he went as a living soul, pausing by the rose garden we helped our parents dig when we were only children. I try to avoid looking at the new cottages—I prefer remembering things as once they were."

"Then Willy is . . . is . . ." I couldn't even say the word.

Miss Blakley patted my shoulders gently.

"So you have seen him," she said in a quiet voice. "It is said he walks sometimes, but there have been no reports of any glimpses of him for a few decades now. But you have seen him." She smiled, then looked anxiously in my face. "Was he well? Did he seem happy?"

"I can show you," I said, picking my sketchbook up from the ground.

It was both wonderful and awful when old Miss Blakley looked down at the portrait of her brother; luckily it was in the pad I'd brought with me. Looking at her, then at the full-size portrait I'd done of Willy, made the resemblance between the two more obvious—the same green eyes, the same curve of the cheek. I could tell Miss Blakley was fighting back tears. It might have been easier if she'd cried.

"Did you speak?" she asked in a hushed voice.

I bowed my head, feeling somehow embarrassed.

I nodded.

"Willy told me he checked up on you from time to time," I told her.

Old Miss Blakley smiled, a smile much like her brother's. Then she clapped her hands.

"I knew it!" she cried. "I have felt him many times, though I myself have never seen him. I often feel him in the rose garden, where we used to pick roses even though we weren't allowed. I would always open and close the gates most carefully while Willy simply leapt right over."

"He still does!"

"May I?" she asked, looking down at the portrait which I held in my hands, then back up at me.

"Of course," I answered, carefully removing the portrait from my sketch pad and presenting it to her.

"This is the most wonderful gift I have received in seventy years," she said, looking again at her brother's happy, beaming face. "I have so wanted to see his smile once again."

"He said you were a rare one," I said, remembering Willy's exact words.

"Thank you, my dear. Thank you."

Miss Blakley patted my shoulder again.

I could tell she wanted to be alone.

I was turning to go when Miss Blakley called me by my name.

"Leah," she said, "one thing more."

"Yes?"

Miss Blakley smiled.

"It is good luck, or so the locals say."

"What is good luck?"

"Seeing Willy brings good luck. They say that around Westfleet and time has proven it true."

I walked home slowly, quietly, thoughtfully, feeling both sad and happy, and believing what Miss Blakley had told me, because I already felt it inside. And if just seeing Willy brings good luck, imagine what kissing him will do. Even the sea wind, blowing through the scrub pines, soft as Willy's kiss, seemed to whisper in my ear that I was unlucky no longer.

Leah

BEFORE
THANKS-
GIVING

FROM THE DIARY OF
SHARON CREADY

he only thing bad in my life is this dumb diary. I know some people think keeping a diary is really cool, but I'm not one of them. I think they're a major waste of time. I know they're supposed to be great if you want to be a writer, but I don't want to be a writer. I'd rather *tell* my friends all the great things going on in my life than spend time writing them down!

The only things *I'm* excited about writing are the invitations to my wedding. I know it's not so romantic, but Louie proposed over the telephone. I said yes (of course!) and Louie promised that when we're together over Thanksgiving he'll propose on his bended knee. I can't wait. He's so cute and I know we're going to be happy together in a major way. I don't think we're too young or anything. After all, I've known him for a long time—we started dating in eleventh grade and we've been together ever since.

That's the reason I hate college—I miss Louie all the time. I really miss him, even though I've got good friends here, especially Bobbie and Lene. That's short for Ilene, and Bobbie is short for Roberta. They're kind of dumb names if you ask me, but they're really cool girls. I'm lucky, 'cause this term we got to share a suite. I'm glad I didn't get put in a single like a lot of girls wanted. I hate being alone. Bobbie and Lene say they're going to really miss me next term, and I'll miss them, too. I love talking with them. In fact, I just love talking. I hate silence. Anyway, I'm not coming back to South Central University. No way. Once Louie and I break the news to Mom and Dad, I'm going to tell them I'm transferring to the state school near Ridgefield. I've already been accepted, and the good part is I can go part-time. The rest of the time I can work, so Louie and I can rent a little apartment in Ridgefield and have money to go out for fancy dinners. That's what Louie and I love doing—going out for romantic dinners in some candlelit restaurant and toasting each other with champagne, or at least wine. I can't wait.

I can already imagine how I'm going to decorate our apartment. Louie says it's all up to me—I'm the one with good taste. He says the only thing he has good taste in is women, and that's why he chose me. He says we're going to be so happy together they'll write books about us! I can't wait. I know I said it before, but it's true. Bobbie and Lene promise to visit. Sometimes I think maybe they're kind of tired of hearing about Louie and me, and maybe I *do* talk about Louie too much, but I can't help it. Louie is *so* cute, especially his nose and that cleft chin. I never knew I liked cleft chins so much until I met Louie. I didn't know I liked red hair either. (Louie's a redhead.) Bobbie asked if he had a brother, and Lene wants me to try to clone him!

It's Tuesday and that means tomorrow we get to go home for Thanksgiving. Yes! It's a two-hour express train ride to Albany, then I change for the train to Ridgefield. I'll go straight to Louie's apartment before I go to Mom and Dad's. Louie didn't go to college like me, but that's cool. Not everybody has to go to school. I mean, Louie already has a good job, working for his family's insulation company. He's making a decent salary and he's going to get more soon. His dad wants him to work his way up the ranks so when he's older and runs the company he'll know everything about it. That means when we're older and have kids and all that, Louie will be president of Collins Incorporated and we'll get to live in a nice house right in Ridgefield, right near Mom and Dad. And our kids can go to Ridgefield Elementary, just like I did. I loved that school. I had such great teachers, except for Mrs. Manton. But she's not there anymore, so that's good. Everything's going to be just great. More than great. Perfect.

All I have to do is get through this term and then, come Christmas, I'll be home free. Louie and me. We're going to get married on New Year's Day. Just a small wedding, that's all we want. Bobbie and Lene will be my bridesmaids. But I have to pass all my courses here to still be accepted in

Hopperton State. That's why I'm working so hard on this dumb diary. Mr. Highsmith says to pass English our diaries have to be at least fifty pages. So far mine's only seventeen. I kind of forgot about it those weekends I went home to visit Louie. That's why I'm catching up now. Mr. Highsmith said he didn't care if we wrote the entire thing the last three days of the semester, the important thing was that we wrote. I hope you remember that, Mr. Highsmith! It's fifty pages or bust! I figure if I write every spare moment I'll make at least fifty. I want to do well so Louie will be proud of me. Of course, he says he's proud of me already, but I want him to be even prouder now *and* in the future!

You know, writing in this diary isn't as bad as I thought it would be. I'm kind of pretending I'm talking, except on paper. You know how much I like to chat, don't you, Mr. Highsmith? I hope you've forgiven me for all the times I interrupted class by talking to Bobbie or Lene when I shouldn't have. But if I have something on my mind, I just let it out. Louie says I better not ever commit a crime (as if I ever would!), because right away I'd tell the cops I'd done it. I'm the worst liar in the world, I really am.

Tuesday, November 23rd—later on

Bobbie just came in and asked how come I was still writing in this diary if I hate it so much. I said I was liking it a bit more. Then I said, "Anything for an A!" (That's a hint, Mr. Highsmith!) She was all excited because she, Lene, and I are getting a ride home for Thanksgiving with three other girls from the dorm. Yes! The gas split six ways will be a lot cheaper than taking the train. I can take the money I'll save and buy a little something for Louie. They'll drop me off in Hopperton, which is around twenty miles from Ridgefield, so Louie can come pick me up. It'll be fun. We can blast music the whole way. Bobbie says that Carole (she's the girl giving us the ride) has a major sound system in her car and likes to use it. I love loud music, and so does Louie. Our first purchase is going to be a super CD player with a five-disc changer so we won't have to even get up and change the music for four hours at a time, if you know what I mean. (Sorry, Mr. Highsmith, I hope you're not a prude!) Louie and I even like the same kinds of music, so that's good. Lene's boyfriend only likes house music and she hates it. She's retro. She says they argue about it round the clock. Louie and I almost never argue. I can't believe how lucky I am. I mean, it's not as though I'm the best person in the world or anything, and everything's working out perfect. What was that song—"The Future's So Bright I Gotta Wear Shades"? I think that was it. That could be my theme song—me and Louie.

•   •   •

Tuesday, November 23rd—after dinner

Major cool! Bobbie, Lene, and I had dinner with Carole. Her car's a Lexus, so I'll be going in style. She pointed out the two other girls coming with us from across the cafeteria—Jeannie and Eliza. They're okay. Jeannie's in my Chem class and Eliza's in Anthropology. Carole asked us if we minded making one stop on the way to the Interstate. She wants to see Luvia! Bobbie and I have talked about doing that for the past two terms, but since we didn't have a car, we never got around to doing it. It's so great to be going to Luvia right before Thanksgiving when Louie and I announce our engagement and everything. It's weird that Lene hadn't heard about Luvia—but she always has her head in the clouds, I guess. Luvia is only the most major psychic in the whole state. I mean, I thought *everyone* at South Central had heard of her. Everyone knows the story of the senior who went to Luvia at midterm and said she was going to drop out. Luvia said she'd be crazy to drop out, and if she stayed in school she'd get a major amount of money. The girl thought like yeah, but she did what Luvia said. And three weeks later her great-uncle dropped dead and in his will he left her all this money—like a lot—but only if she was either still in school or had graduated from college. So she got big bucks, thanks to Luvia. I can't believe I'm going to get to see her.

The way it works is that first she reads your palm, then she sits and thinks or something for a few minutes, then she says what she sees, then you get to ask her seven questions. Mine are all going to be about Louie and me and our future. I mean, it's not that I'm worried about it or anything, I just want to know all the good stuff ahead of time. Like how many kids we'll have. Also where we'll live. That kind of thing. I mean, I know my future is going to be totally cool, but I also want someone else to tell me so, too. It's like when I was a kid—even when I got a 100% on a spelling test, I wasn't happy unless my teacher put a big gold star on top of the page. I don't see what's so wrong about that. Anyway, I bet Luvia's going to smile when she looks at my palm and just say, "Totally cool future," or something like that, and Lene and Bobbie and Carole and Jeannie and Eliza will turn green with jealousy. I'd be jealous of me if I weren't me already. Carole said she'd made the appointment with Luvia in September—that's how in demand she is. God—I hope there'll be time for all of us to see her! I hadn't thought of that before. I hope Carole reserved a big chunk of time. Carole says the sessions take fifteen minutes each, so that means one and a half hours total. That means I'll get home a lot later than I would if I took the train. Bobbie says if she were going home to her boyfriend, she'd skip Luvia and take the train, just to see him that much earlier. But I want to see Luvia and ask my seven questions. Maybe with so many of us, we'll only get to ask five questions. That's okay. I just decided I really want to know if our first child is going to be a boy or a girl. Louie wants a girl so she'll look just like me. I kind of want a girl, too, so I can dress her up. But I don't really care because Louie and I are going to be so happy together it won't really matter. I just remembered what Louie told me on the phone—he said no one could ever replace me, I was that special, and we'd be together forever.

Now I'm wondering all of a sudden what Luvia looks like. I bet she's ugly with lots of hairy warts. God—I hope she can't read minds! What if she knows what I just wrote and tells me mean things! It's all your fault, Mr. Highsmith, if she makes up mean stuff about my future!

Wednesday, November 24th—6:30 A.M.!

I'm so excited I can't sleep, so I figured I might as well get in a few paragraphs before breakfast. If I get writer's cramp and die, you're the one to blame, Mr. Highsmith! But who cares! Today I get to see Louie and kiss him and—well, I'm not going to write *everything!* Louie will think it's a waste of money to visit Luvia, but I won't tell him about it until later. I mean, when I first woke up I almost decided to take the train so I'd see Louie a bit earlier. I was about to tell Bobbie I wasn't going to go with her, but if I did that I wouldn't learn about my future! I know—maybe I'll write down what Luvia says and then show it to Louie when it comes true. Then I'll get to see him wrinkle up his cute nose the way he does when he finds out he's wrong about something. He *hates* being wrong about anything. He won't ever admit he's wrong, but he will wrinkle up his little nose so then I know he knows he's wrong and it's so cute it makes me love him even more.

Wednesday, November 24th—at Luvia's

My mother would have a cow if she saw this place! It's this old wooden house that hasn't been painted or cleaned or even swept since I don't know when. I think I counted nine cats, but I'm not sure. And this sofa I have to wait on is gross—covered with cat hair and I don't even like to guess what else! But Carole just whispered that it'll be worth the wait. Yup, you guessed it, Mr. Highsmith—I go last. Since there are six of us, Luvia said to do it alphabetically by our middle names. Of course mine would have to be Yvonne! Wait till I get my hands on my Aunt Yvonne! Why couldn't her name have been Abigail, then I'd have gotten to go first. I hate sitting around just waiting. I like doing things, not thinking about them. If I think too long I start to feel kind of worried or something and not feel so sure about things anymore. I'm a doer, that's what I am. But now I'm a waiter. Luvia said she won't answer less than seven questions—seven must be a magic number or something—so that means I'll be waiting one hour and fifteen minutes without an interruption, stuck in the middle of this pigsty! But at least it will give me time to write more in this diary and think about seeing Louie again. I'd be with him just around now if I'd taken the train. I wish I had. But I'll have a funny story to tell him about my day. Wait till he hears about me sitting on a grimy sofa surrounded by peacock feathers and hourglasses and crystal balls and weird velvet drapes. If it wasn't drizzling I'd take a walk. Luvia didn't look the way I'd imagined her. She's pretty regular-looking—middle-aged, a little overweight, brown hair going gray, a few wrinkles. If she'd let me redo her hair and take her shopping she wouldn't look too bad. She also needs a major cleaning! Her fingernails aren't exactly clean! Oh God! I forgot she might be able to read minds! But if she could read minds, then she'd have known our middle names without even asking. I never knew Lene's middle name was Lucille! Gross! Sorry, Lene—but Ilene Lucille Lubello isn't exactly elegant! I mean— Whoa, here comes Bobbie. Roberta Ann. Wow! She looks happy. I gotta stop writing.

Wednesday, November 24th—a little later, still at Luvia's

Wow! I'm impressed. Bobbie says Luvia took her hand, meditated for a minute or so, and then said Bobbie's mom had been sick but she saw her recovering in the future. And Bobbie's mom *has* been sick! She also said she saw unhappiness with a "love interest." That's true, too—Bobbie's boyfriend, Wolf, is a major pain. I mean, at first I thought he was nice, 'cause that's how he acts. But he's not really that way, not once you actually get to know him. So what did Bobbie ask Luvia about her future? we wanted to know, the rest of us girls except for Carole—Carole Jane, that is, who's now in with Luvia. Bobbie kind of blushed and said she'd asked if she'd get married. Luvia said yes, and pretty soon, to a man with red hair (weird—Bobbie usually can't stand redheads!) she knew of but hadn't met (whatever that means). Luvia said he and Bobbie would help each other overcome a "terrible tragedy" and that this would lead to love and marriage. Now I really can't wait to see Luvia and hear about *my* future!

Wednesday, November 24th—STILL at Luvia's

Now Lene, Carole, and Eliza have gone, too. Jeannie's in there now. I'm next. Lene said she'd kill me if I wrote down what she asked. Sorry, Mr. Highsmith. You can ask her yourself if you really want to know! I'm next. It's going to be worth the wait, I know it is. Anything about Louie and me and our future is going to be sweet.

Wednesday, November 24th—in the car

Am I pissed! For once this dumb diary's coming in useful. Lene and Bobbie and Carole and Jeannie and Eliza are sick of hearing me gripe. "Sharon, enough already!" said dumb

Carole. "It's my car, so stop complaining and listen to the music." It's hard to write in a moving car, even if it is a Lexus. Sorry, Mr. Highsmith, if you can't read my writing too easily, but it's not my fault. And I'm angling this notebook up so that nosy Eliza can't read what I'm writing. It's a good thing I'm up against the door, so there's only a person on one side of me. I don't want Lene and Bobbie to read about how dumb I think they are. Jerks. I mean, I would have stood up for them if it had been the other way around.

Here's what happened, so you can decide for yourself, Mr. Highsmith. And I bet you'll agree with me. Jeannie came out and it was my turn, so I went in. I sat down, and Luvia took my hand. Her hand really was pretty gross, but I kept thinking to myself, "Nice hand, nice hand," in case she really could read minds. (Eliza just asked what I was writing, so I told her to mind her own business.) Anyway, all of a sudden Luvia dropped my hand like it was made of lava or something, and clutched her head. "Oh," she says, "I've got this awful headache. It's so terrible." "So?" I say. "I'm sorry and all, but let's hear about my future and stuff." "No," says Luvia, "my head hurts too much. I can't concentrate. I don't usually do this many readings in a row. I guess it was too much." I was thinking if she's such a good psychic, she should have known that ahead of time. "C'mon," I say, "just answer me a few questions. You can give short answers, I don't care." But Luvia just looked at me with this weird expression. I hadn't noticed she really was pretty weird-looking. "No," she says, "my head hurts too much. I just can't." I started to complain again, but Luvia says, "You have to go." That's when I got pissed. "No," I say, "I've been waiting all this time and it's Thanksgiving and then when I come back I'll be real busy, then I'm transferring, so I won't get a chance to come again. I want to know stuff now. I mean it. I'm not going to go till you tell me something about my future." Louie always says I can be as stubborn as a mule when I want to be, and maybe even that dumb Luvia noticed I wasn't going to budge until she told me something. "All right," she finally says, "here's what I'm going to do. I'm going to write something about your future on a piece of paper, and fold it up and seal it in an envelope." "A fat lot of good that'll do me," I say. "You can read it when you get home," Luvia finally says. That was okay, although I didn't act too thrilled. I was thinking it would be fun to sit in Louie's arms and open it together, but I didn't let on. I wanted Luvia to feel bad for making me wait so long for nothing. So Luvia walked across the room to this really messy desk and wrote something. I couldn't see what she'd written, since she was standing in the way. But it couldn't have been much, since it only took a few seconds. Then she put it in an envelope like she'd said and licked it. Then she watched while I put it in my pocketbook, and made me promise not to read it till I got home. Then she walked me into the waiting room and told everybody she'd gotten this really bad headache (though she didn't look that sick to me), and that she'd given me something to read when I got home. Then she made everyone promise not to let me read it till I got home, and they all said they would. I thought at least Bobbie or Lene would tell Luvia it wasn't fair to make me wait so long for so little, but for once they kept their big mouths shut. Maybe I won't ask them to be bridesmaids at my wedding. Maybe I'll invite that awful Becky Sue Anderson and throw the bouquet so she catches it. That would *kill* Bobbie and Lene! Anyway, of course I wanted to look at the paper the second we got in the car, but they wouldn't let me. And Bobbie's been keeping an eye on me to make sure I don't peek. Lene just said she bet Luvia knew I'd won the lottery (Louie plays our lucky numbers every Wednesday) and she didn't want me to get too excited before I got home, so Louie and I could celebrate together. That sounds good. Carole says Luvia saw that Louie had already found the perfect apartment and she didn't want to ruin the surprise, and since my future is going to be so perfect anyway, there wasn't much to say. Of course it is, I know it is. Bobbie said she'd seen that photo of Louie I have in our suite, and if *her* future included one night with him, that would be all she'd need to know, even if he *is* a redhead. At first I thought they were just trying to humor me so I won't start complaining again. But I guess they really are right—I *am* the luckiest girl in the car. Who knows when any of them will meet someone like Louie who really loves them like Louie loves me? Especially Bobbie—she's *never* lucky when it comes to love. I mean, at first I was kind of scared when Luvia weirded out—like maybe she knew that Louie didn't love me anymore. But I know that's not true. I know it. Louie loves me and I love him. I wish I'd never bothered with Luvia and had just gone straight home on the train. Well, that doesn't matter—we're almost to Hopperton and no harm done. Now I think I'll take a little snooze so I'm fresh for Louie later on, then we can open the envelope together and read about the future.

From the
South Central University Sentinel,
Wednesday, December 1st

The South Central University Sentinel is grieved to have to report the death of a popular sophomore, Sharon Cready, in a freak car accident on the way home for Thanksgiving vacation on Wednesday, November 24. According to authorities, Ms. Cready fell asleep while traveling in a car driven by Carole Oakwood, also an S.C.U. sophomore, and somehow managed to lean against the door handle, causing the door to open, thereby causing Ms. Cready (who was not wearing a seat belt) to fall out of the speeding vehicle onto Rte. 95, near the town of Hopperton, only miles from Ms. Cready's hometown of Ridgefield. Death was instantaneous. By Ms. Cready's body were a notebook containing a diary and a pocketbook containing a sealed envelope. None of Ms. Cready's companions, all of whom were unhurt, was willing to provide an explanation for the brief note contained in the envelope: on a slip of paper, in purple ink, were written two words: "No Future."

hey say most only children are un-
happy when their new sibling is first
brought home from the hospital, and I
was no exception. But at least I had a
good reason: *my* little sister was so little I couldn't even see her.

Even now, three years later, I can remember the day well.

It was July and I was seven years old. I had just finished
second grade and had been the best reader in the class.
Back in late winter, when I'd first learned Momma was
pregnant, I had tried to find some books in our school library about babies and all that. I like being well informed.
But when I asked for help finding them, the librarian gave
me an odd look and called me precocious. I don't imagine
she thought I knew what precocious meant. But I did. And
not only was I precocious enough to understand the word,
I also already knew a thing or two about babies.

For one thing, I knew they didn't have to have fathers,
no matter what anyone said. *I* didn't have a father, and I'm
still here. I mean, I knew a father was necessary at the very
beginning. It just wasn't necessary for him to stay in the
picture. I also knew that when women go to the hospital to

have babies, they tend to go in the middle of the night and then stay there for a few days.

At least that's the way it was when I was born.

Not that I remember this myself, but that's what Grandmother told me.

She's my mother's mother, of course. Remember—I don't have a father. Neither does my mother, but for a different reason: her father died. Momma says if Grandmother had been more alert to the signs, it never would have happened. That made me wonder if Momma's father had been killed in a car crash when Grandmother was driving, but Momma said don't be ridiculous, she wasn't talking about road signs. I suppose I should have figured that out for myself—Momma *hates* road signs. She says she'll only believe in road signs if the person who put them up had to sign them at the bottom. That way, if they were incorrect, you'd have someone to complain to. Momma says it's no coincidence that you never see them putting up road signs during the day—they seem to sneak them up at night when no one's around. Maybe that's why Momma dislikes driving so much.

Anyway, back to my grandmother. She got married again when I was five and I had to be the ring bearer at her wedding.

Grandmother's two favorite stories are how I almost lost the ring at her wedding and how Momma almost had me at the movies.

What happened was, when Momma was nine and one

half months pregnant she went off to a double feature and missed the ending of the second movie because she had to be rushed to the hospital to have me.

Momma says I came shooting out like a rocket but that she had to stay in the hospital four days anyway. I don't think that that could have been much fun for me. I was dumped in one of those nurseries you are always seeing on television, except I didn't have any visitors cooing at me through the glass because Momma told no one where she was. She didn't even bother to phone Grandmother—she must have thought Momma was still at the movies.

So that's how I know mothers usually spend a few days in the hospital after giving birth—from personal experience. And that's why when Momma told me I was going to have my new brother or sister very soon now, I started wondering where I would stay when she went into the hospital.

I didn't think I'd be sent to Grandmother's. For one thing, Grandmother now lived over four hours away and Momma didn't want to drive that far. (Remember, Momma hates driving.) And secondly, Momma and Grandmother weren't even talking. They'd had a terrible argument the Christmas before. It had to do with Momma's father, I think. When I asked Momma what Grandmother had done that was so mean, she explained it was what Grandmother *hadn't* done that was the meanest of all. "What people refrain from doing often has more effect than what they actually do," Momma told me after Christmas. I didn't quite understand what she meant, but I acted as if I did. Momma gets upset when she thinks I don't understand her, because she says I'm the only person left who really does. So I act as though I do, even if I don't, because I hate it when Momma's unhappy. Anyway, Momma and Grandmother hadn't spoken since, although Grandmother did send me five dollars for my birthday in April. I wasn't even sure Grandmother knew where we were living since we'd moved.

Just when I was starting to get really worried about where I'd stay, Momma explained that having babies was different than it was only seven years ago, and if there were no complications, mother and child were sent home the very day of the birth.

I didn't know what Momma meant by "complications," but I asked her anyway what would happen if there were any.

"The doctor says everything is fine," said Momma happily. "So I don't expect there'll be any."

Then I wanted to know what would happen if the baby arrived late at night, the way I had. I vaguely recalled hearing children under twelve were banned from hospitals. Being only seven, I didn't like the idea of spending a night in our apartment all by myself. New York City can be a pretty scary place to be alone when you're still a kid, especially if you've just moved there and haven't met anyone yet. Momma said I'd meet more people than I ever wanted to once school started up in September, and anyway, explained

Momma, these days you could induce labor if you wanted to.

Even a good reader who's only seven years old couldn't be expected to know what *that* meant, so Momma told me she could just make an appointment with her doctor once her nine months were up, go to the hospital, take some sort of drug, and then the baby would be born.

"So," said Momma, "this means I can go to the hospital first thing in the morning and be back in time for supper. I'll have it ready beforehand and you can put it in the oven and heat it up for when the baby and I get home."

That was precisely the way it happened.

On Tuesday morning, the second of July, a fresh, windy morning, Momma took a casserole from the freezer and set it out to thaw on the kitchen counter.

"Today is the day," she said, and at first I thought she meant she'd finally decided to serve the string bean casserole she'd been saving for a day when we felt extra hungry and the weather was cool enough to really enjoy it. Then I figured out it was the day for the baby to come.

Momma told me to put the casserole in the oven at four-fifteen and bake it at 350 degrees for an hour. That way it would be ready when she and the baby came home at five-fifteen. She even showed me how to set the oven to 350, which I already knew. Then she said if she'd be much later she'd call, gave me a kiss, and told me not to open the door to strangers or anyone else for that matter, even our building's super. Momma says Mr. Mikula has the brains of an overboiled turnip, although she likes his son, Vladimir.

Then she left.

It was a long day. I couldn't watch television because Momma had thrown ours in the trash one day when she hadn't liked the show she was watching. So I read for an hour or two and when I got tired of that I made myself a peanut butter and jelly sandwich for lunch when it was only ten forty-five; then I drew for a few hours and finally ended up taking a nap on the sofa. Luckily some people shouting in the street woke me up in time to put the casserole in the oven by a quarter past four. I also set the dining room table with our best silver and Momma's favorite dishes. Even though I knew babies didn't eat at tables, I set a place for my new brother or sister.

Then I waited some more.

At five-fifteen on the dot, the door opened and in stepped Momma.

"It's a girl," she said. "So you've got a sister! And I've named her Lily."

Momma looked very happy, but the weird thing was she wasn't holding any baby. I peered behind her in the hall, in case the baby was there, being carried by a nurse or something, but the hall was empty except for a trash bag by someone's door. There didn't seem to be a baby anywhere. The only thing Momma was holding, besides her pocketbook, was one of those Styrofoam cups you order take-out coffee in.

"Where's the baby?" I wanted to know.

"Her name's Lily, dear, and she's right here in this coffee cup."

Momma must have seen my jaw drop because she quickly added, "There's no coffee in there, you silly! It's a clean, dry cup and this little plastic cover has a hole in it so Lily can breathe. I was concerned that if I tried to carry her in my arms, the way I brought you home from the hospital, she might just blow away. And she's so tiny I didn't know if I'd be able to find her again."

I didn't know what to say. I knew premature babies were sometimes terribly small, but I knew this baby hadn't been premature: Momma had waited nine months before inducing labor. Then I became worried that Momma had got the dates wrong: she wasn't especially good with numbers. What if she'd told the doctor it was nine months but it was only two or three? But wouldn't a doctor know that kind of thing? I wasn't even sure how much weight Momma had gained (I knew pregnant women gain weight) because Momma only wears loose-fitting clothes, like long sweeping robes. She says she has no desire to appear like some organ-grinder's monkey, attired in tight pantaloons.

I was still trying to figure this out when Momma asked if I'd like to take a look at my new sister.

Very carefully she removed the plastic cover and lowered the cup down in front of me.

"Don't blow on her, dear," Momma told me. "She's so little it would be like you or me being hit by a gale-force wind."

I looked in the cup and it was absolutely empty. There was nothing in it. I didn't know what to say.

Momma was watching my face closely and I could tell she was disappointed by what she saw.

She quickly snatched the cup away and replaced the cover.

"I was afraid this might happen," she said. "I suppose you couldn't even see your own sister."

"But there's nothing there," I replied.

Momma shook her head impatiently.

"I will grant you," she said slowly, "that your sister Lily *is* an exceptionally small baby, but she *is* most definitely there. Would you care to try again?"

I nodded. The cover came off and the cup was placed right in front of my face. I desperately wanted to see something, but I couldn't. All I saw was an empty cup.

Momma looked saddened but undaunted.

"Never mind for now," she said. "The time will come."

She then went to her bedroom and returned with an old wooden jewelry box. Dumping her jewelry into a plastic bag, Momma next lined the box with some soft material.

"If I'd known beforehand how small Lily was going to be," she explained as she worked, "I'd have had this ready earlier. The crib I bought is just too huge for such a tiny baby. We'll simply have to change our way of thinking when it comes to Lily."

Momma then transferred Lily from the coffee cup to the jewelry box—not that *I* could see her, of course.

"This is where Lily shall stay," Momma announced. "Needless to say, you are not to play with the box or disturb it in any manner whatsoever. If you wish to see your sister, or hold her, ask me first. We can't be too careful with a child this small."

While I removed the casserole from the oven, Momma went and rummaged around for something in the bathroom.

"Thank goodness," she said happily, entering the kitchen, holding something gingerly in her left hand. For a moment I thought it was Lily and that I could see my sister, but it turned out to be an eyedropper.

"I knew I had one somewhere," Momma said as she carefully rinsed out the eyedropper, "and I was right. It's also in good shape. This saves me a trip to the pharmacy," she added cheerfully. Then her expression got serious. "I'd hate to have to go out and leave you alone with Lily," she went on, "especially since you can't even see her."

This made me feel unhappy, and when I'm unhappy I tend to get all quiet. I guess I'm kind of like Momma in that way. But the night Lily came home, curiosity got the better of me.

"What's the eyedropper for?" I wanted to know.

"To feed Lily with, of course. She's much too little to use a bottle. Neither would she be able to breast-feed. This eyedropper might even be too large, but I can't think what else to use."

From the cabinet right above the refrigerator Momma produced a box of formula and started preparing it.

"I breast-fed you," Momma explained as she was stirring

the mixture. "Mother's milk is much better than formula. I'm sure it helped you grow up so quickly and be so big and strong."

I figured if anyone needed help growing up quickly and being big and strong, it was Lily.

"So what are you going to do about it?" I demanded.

"About what?" wondered Momma, testing the formula on her wrist to make sure it was the right temperature.

"About feeding Lily mother's milk since it's so much better for her."

"I'll have to buy an extractor," Momma replied, then explained what an extractor was. She looked thoughtful for a moment and then, in sort of a cold tone, she added, "Well, at least I'm glad to hear you believe Lily exists, even if you can't see her yet."

I blushed right up to my ears and felt miserable. I didn't even know if I thought Lily existed. No book I'd ever read had mentioned a baby being too small to see and I couldn't recall ever hearing about that kind of thing on the television. I wished Momma hadn't thrown ours out: teeny-tiny babies and what to do with them were just the sort of topic they might discuss on those talk shows I used to watch on the days when I was sick and could stay home from school. I resolved to find out where the nearest library was and do some research on very small children.

By the color of my ears Momma knew I was embarrassed and didn't really believe in Lily. She gave a sigh, and with the eyedropper now filled with formula, went into the dining room where Lily lay in the jewelry box. When Momma's angry or disappointed with me, she can act as though I've suddenly become invisible. She'll keep it up until she either forgets she's supposed to be angry or else just suddenly forgives me.

"That's a good girl," I heard Momma say from where I stood in the kitchen. Just as I was going into the dining room to watch, Momma returned to the kitchen, proudly waving the empty eyedropper in front of her.

"She drank every last drop!" she boasted.

Of course I suspected Momma of having downed the formula herself, but I kept my mouth shut. And when Momma was rinsing out the eyedropper, I did peer once again into the jewelry box, but as far as I could tell, the only thing in it was the material Momma had put on the bottom.

"Diapers," Momma suddenly said as we were eating the casserole that night. Lily was asleep, or so said Momma, and her jewelry box crib was out of harm's way on top of the bookcase in the small passage between the living and dining rooms. I looked up from my plate, where I'd been engaged in trying to cut a string bean so tough I was wondering if it could be a twig, when Momma continued:

"Yes—diapers are the problem we now face."

"What do you mean?"

"I mean they do not make diapers in Lily's size, and diapers she must have. You did. All babies do. I will not have Lily doing without simply because she is not as large as people think babies ought to be."

While I chewed the twiglike string bean I considered this new dilemma. It seemed to me a baby that microscopic—if indeed a baby was actually there—would hardly require diapers, but I kept that thought to myself.

"How about doll's clothing?" I at last suggested. "I'm sure they make diapers for dolls."

Momma shook her head impatiently.

"Really," she said, "for an intelligent child you sometimes make me wonder! Tell me—have you ever seen a doll as small as Lily?"

I'd never even seen Lily, so the question was a bit silly. I just shook my head and remained silent.

"Well," said Momma finally, "I shall simply have to buy cloth and make them myself. But it won't be easy. They will have to be terribly small. And washing them will be no easy task, either: they'll have to be done by hand, of course—in a washing machine they'd just vanish away."

I would have suggested they be disposable, but Momma doesn't believe in disposability, with the sole exception of television sets.

So the summer passed, with July soon being engulfed by August. As we lived directly across from Gramercy Park, my days were spent playing there. Momma's days were spent watching Lily, who still remained invisible to my eyes.

With her usual ingenuity, Momma had contrived to attach a long ribbon to Lily's jewelry box crib. Momma would then tie the ribbon around her thin neck in such a manner that the jewelry box would rest on her breasts. Thus Momma could take Lily with her when she went shopping, even though it earned her some pretty strange looks. I wasn't allowed to baby-sit because, as Momma put it, how could I be expected to watch something I couldn't even see?

I soon discovered the location of the local library and began my research. I quickly learned more about babies than I'll ever need to know—but still could find no information about children so small as to be invisible. After repeated visits, I mustered my courage to approach the librarian, a steely woman with pointy glasses, coarse gray hair streaked with white, and a severe expression. The nameplate on her desk read "Mrs. Manton."

"I'm studying babies," I told her, "especially ones that are small."

"Most babies are," she replied.

"I mean *really* small," I persisted.

"Perhaps you mean premature babies," she stated. "They tend to be small. But perhaps you don't know what a premature baby is."

I saw immediately I'd have to impress her with my knowledge of babies; she was not the type of grown-up who can see children for what they really are without a bit of assistance.

"No," I said somewhat grandly, "while I do know what premature babies are, this is not what I'm wondering about.

I'm actually seeking material on babies whose birth was induced after the pregnancy ran its full term."

Her eyebrows shot up. She appeared to realize I knew my stuff.

"No," I continued, "I am interested in learning about babies who happen to be amazingly small."

"How small?" she wanted to know. "Under a pound?"

"Smaller," I replied.

"Half a pound?"

"Smaller yet," I answered.

"An ounce?"

"Keep on going."

"We are, are we not, talking about *human* babies?" she inquired.

"We are talking about my sister," I informed her.

"You have a sister who weighs less than an ounce?" she asked, staring at me.

"A lot less," I told her.

"Impossible!" she snorted, then fixed me with her narrow eyes. "I am a busy woman," she said, "and have better things to do than play games with overimaginative children."

She then stared at some dull-looking papers on her desk, this to indicate our discussion was at an end.

"People who don't know anything would be well advised to keep their mouths firmly shut," I told her, repeating verbatim one of Momma's favorite expressions.

"Well I never!" she gasped as I took my leave.

I never went back to that library and I also never told

Momma what had happened there. After all, the librarian didn't even know my name, so there was no way of her causing me any trouble, such as calling up Momma to complain. The thing was, you see, that Momma was very secretive about Lily.

"It isn't that I'm not proud of her," she told me one afternoon in August. "It's simply that I know how unkind people can be: they stare, make uncalled-for remarks, and heaven knows what else. And, while babies may not understand word for word what is said to them, I'm convinced they are susceptible to the sentiments the words express, and I refuse to have Lily subjected to such abuse. A child as special as she has enough of a hard row to hoe without others planting weeds in her garden."

Momma likes comparing things to plants, even though we had none in our apartment. "What if I had one and it died?" she would ask. "I don't believe I could bear it."

Momma's mood that summer varied with Lily's progress. And by progress she meant growth: physical growth. Each afternoon when I returned from the park, Momma would meet me at the apartment door. On good days she'd smile and say, "Things are looking up—she'll be just fine in no time." But on the bad days Momma would shake her head darkly and murmur, "No growth."

I kept attempting to see my sister but still saw nothing. A few times the bottom of the jewelry box did seem slightly damp. This I took as a hopeful sign that Lily's diapers had leaked, and thus concrete evidence of her existence. But it was also possible that Momma had let slip some milk when she was fussing with the eyedropper—I couldn't be sure, because Momma liked feeding Lily in private.

"Why do you want to watch, anyway?" she'd demand. "You can't see her."

September arrived and with it school. I was glad to go. I loved Momma, but sometimes I felt nervous around the apartment. I both disbelieved in Lily yet at the same time was scared I might step on her by mistake.

Momma met me at the apartment door when the first day of school was over. But instead of asking me about my teacher (too fat) or the other kids (too many) or the work (too easy), she dissolved into tears.

"She's gone!" she gasped. "Lily's gone. I've lost her!"

At first I wasn't sure whether Momma meant Lily had died or was just mislaid. Luckily it was the latter: a strong gust of wind had knocked over a vase containing dried weeds, which in turn had knocked Lily's crib off the bookcase that stood between the living and dining rooms.

"And oh," cried Momma, "I ran in and saw her little crib on the floor but couldn't find her anywhere! I've been looking for hours!"

I was too embarrassed to suggest Momma check the soles of her shoes, but she resolved that doubt for me:

"It may sound macabre," she said, "but I even checked under my shoes—but our baby's nowhere!"

We were standing right by the door, Momma weeping and I not knowing what to do. Momma had said I shouldn't go running into the apartment for fear of squashing the baby.

I didn't want to spend the night in the hall, so I suggested we get on hands and knees and search out specific areas of the apartment; once we were sure Lily wasn't there, these could be our pathways so we could at least get to the bathroom, kitchen, and our bedrooms. Momma was convinced Lily, if anywhere, had to be somewhere in the living or dining rooms, that being where the crib had been at the time of the mishap.

As soon as a path had been cleared for safe travel across the living room, I began widening the search area little by little. Momma meanwhile was doing the same thing in the dining room.

Hope flared brightly at one point, then sputtered out: Momma found the little diapers Lily had been wearing that day, but they were now babyless.

So we kept on searching.

It took close to three hours, but by then we were fairly certain Lily was nowhere on the floor of either room.

Momma lay down to cry but I kept on looking. I had to help. I'd never seen Momma so upset.

I was checking on top of the books on the third shelf of the bookcase when I saw it. I mean I saw her. I mean I finally saw Lily.

She was so beautiful I could see why Momma wanted to

name her Lily—she truly resembled one; her skin was so white, her expression so pure. Her little face seemed trans-fused with light. I was amazed at her beauty as well as being amazed I'd never been able to see her before.

Very gently I placed her in the palm of my hand, on her back, the way I'd read babies like to lie. In form she was ex-actly like a regular baby, the only difference being in her size. Looking up at me, she seemed to put her little head to one side in the most fetching gesture. Her eyes were so small I couldn't even tell what color they were.

How Momma's face lit up when I brought Lily in. I couldn't decide which she was more excited about, Lily being found or my being able to see her.

It was a very happy evening.

I soon discovered something odd: some days I was able to see Lily and some days I wasn't. I couldn't understand why, though Momma suggested maybe some days I just wasn't trying hard enough. Perhaps she was right. But in case she wasn't, and the difficulty was with my vision, I went to the school nurse to have my eyes tested. She per-formed the examination and pronounced my vision 20/20, adding I had particularly sharp sight, both close-up and far away.

"I'd say the only things you might have trouble seeing would be things that aren't there," she said with a laugh.

I didn't find her remark very amusing.

Also, in school I was never certain if I should mention having a sister. Sometimes I forgot and said I had one;

sometimes I claimed I was an only child. Of course I got teased a good deal because of this. No one believed that sometimes you could see something and sometimes you couldn't—even if it might always be there. It was something I couldn't quite explain.

It wasn't hard to see that because of this, my fat teacher decided I was a peculiar child. My fears were confirmed when I was summoned to the school psychologist. After I was seated she produced a drawing of my family I had done in art class. I was a good drawer for my age and had tried to make a realistic picture. Thus, in the drawing, I was the size of a regular child and Momma that of a grown-up. Since I didn't have a father, he of course wasn't in the picture. Lily I had portrayed as being the size of a polka dot (actually she was even smaller).

"Let's talk about your drawing," the psychologist said with a wan smile. "It's a very *nice* drawing."

"Thank you," I replied.

"You can say anything you want with me," she continued, "and I'm sure you will . . . Now—tell me: Why didn't you put your father in your drawing?"

I knew right then that I was in trouble. I'd met more than a few people who didn't like the fact that I had no father. According to Momma this was ridiculous. "How," she would demand, "can someone dislike you for something you don't have? It makes no sense. It would make more sense if you're disliked for having something you shouldn't—such as stolen goods—or for having something truly dislikable—such as a loud dog. But to dislike a person for what he doesn't possess is almost a contradiction in terms. Quite metaphysical, when you come to think about it." I decided against sharing Momma's theories with the psychologist and instead replied with simplicity:

"I didn't put my father in the drawing because I don't have one."

"Not at all?"

"No," I said, "not at all."

Pausing a second, the psychologist then spoke. "Perhaps you mean that your father left you, thus you think of him as being nowhere."

"No, no one is nowhere," I answered, a response which momentarily silenced the psychologist.

"I see," she continued after another slight pause. "Well. Uh, then perhaps you could tell me why you made your sister the size of a dot."

"Because that's how big she is."

"Maybe you just *want* her to be that little," suggested the psychologist. "Lots of children wish their younger sister or brother were as small as a, oh—as a thimble."

"Well I don't. And *my* sister is *smaller* than a thimble. And *I* wish she'd get bigger so I could play with her more. But Momma says everyone has to learn to accept people as they are and if everyone were exactly the same it would be a very dull world."

"I see," came the measured response. "Now—concerning your—uh—sister: Your teacher tells me sometimes you say she's there and sometimes you say she isn't. Do you mean she goes somewhere? Perhaps to *her* father's house?"

"No," I replied. "She doesn't have a father, either. And she doesn't *go* anywhere; she just isn't there. I mean that I can't see her."

The psychologist sat up quite straight.

"What do you mean you can't see her? If she were there, of course you would see her."

"That's not the way it works," I explained patiently. "Sometimes you can't see things that really are there."

"I don't think I quite understand," said the psychologist, trying to take notes in a way that I maybe wouldn't notice. "Could you tell me more?"

I sighed and said, "It's like Momma says: Everybody is somebody, but sometimes people aren't able to see it. That's just the way it is and that's the way it is with Lily."

Momma told me later that the school psychologist had phoned her up, asking all kinds of questions and drawing all sorts of rude conclusions. She even wondered if Momma would care to make an appointment to see her.

"I have better things to do," Momma told me she'd replied, and had then gone on to say that if the psychologist dared question me again without permission, Momma would sue the skirt off her.

"About your daughter Lily," persisted the psychologist. "Yes?"

"Well—I just couldn't help but wonder about her."

"She merely happens to be small for her age," Momma

had replied tersely. "Some people are. People do come in different sizes, you know."

"I see. Well—I look forward to seeing her at school someday."

"That's not too likely," said Momma with great finality. "You are precisely the kind of person who wouldn't be able to."

And with that she hung up the phone. I hate it when anything upsets Momma.

But nice things happened that autumn. In shop class I made Lily a beautiful bed so small it could fit handily in a matchbox. The other children teased me mercilessly when at first I said it was for my sister; I quickly added that it was for my sister to play with.

Initially I'd wanted to make Lily some sort of cage, like the ones Chinese people keep crickets in, but Momma was adamant. "No child of mine," she'd announced, "is ever going to live in a cage. Ever."

At any rate, the bed I made for Lily was constructed of wood which I'd stained a warm chestnut color that served to accent the touches of red in her hair. For, like Lily herself, her hair seemed to be growing rapidly. I soon could see Lily every day, and almost every day Momma would greet me at the door with a smile and say, "I do believe Lily's grown a bit today." We gradually got used to the fact that other people couldn't see her at all, much less see how much she'd grown.

"Perhaps someday," said Momma philosophically. I was starting to find it hard to believe that there'd been a time I hadn't been able to see her myself.

"That just goes to show *you're* growing, too," Momma told me happily.

Soon Lily had graduated to solid food. Although she had grown, she was still so small that a banana, for example, could last her more than two weeks. It hadn't been easy finding a spoon small enough to fit in Lily's mouth. Luckily, Momma met a man at the vegetable market who was a retired metalworker and whose hobby was making silverware for dollhouses.

"Imagine," Momma told him, "that a very small doll had a very small doll—and that this doll had a very small doll. Now: I need a spoon small enough for a doll's doll's doll."

This he was able to provide, and many an evening that autumn Momma, Lily, and I would sit all cozy and warm in our living room. Sometimes Momma would feed Lily and sometimes I would. It turned out that I was better at feeding Lily than Momma was, simply because my hands were smaller.

Thanksgiving came and brought us, as Momma put it, three turkeys instead of only one. The normal turkey was the one

Momma bought at the store; the other two were Grandmother and her husband. Momma was still angry over the fight they'd had the previous Christmas and Grandmother was angry because she hadn't known where Momma and I had been for so long.

It probably shouldn't have been surprising, but neither Grandmother nor her husband were able to see Lily. Momma had the idea that Grandmother's husband didn't see Lily because he just *couldn't,* while Grandmother didn't because she just *wouldn't.*

"I wouldn't even want a grandchild as small as that," she said right before she left, "even if such a thing were possible." She then added something about Momma being certifiable, whatever that means, and not even a fit parent for an invisible child.

"You know," said Momma when we three were alone again, "I think we'll do just fine. Lily will grow as much as she can, and we'll keep on loving her no matter what."

"But Momma," I asked, "do you think Lily will ever grow big enough so other people will be able to see her, too?"

"I don't know," said Momma in a soft voice. "I hope so—but you never can tell about people, and perhaps it's not all that important anyway."

Lily's almost three years old now. I'm ten, and Momma won't say how old she is. Lily's learned to speak, but her voice is so small and birdlike Momma and I sometimes have to use ear trumpets to hear what she's saying, and even then we often disagree about what she's said. Lily's kept on growing, though I don't think anyone but Momma and I can tell. Soon after Grandmother's visit, we moved again. Momma said she didn't want Grandmother showing up unexpectedly, trying to take things that weren't hers. I don't think Grandmother knows where we went—I know I haven't received a birthday or Christmas present since we moved. Actually, we've moved twice since then—first to a small town called Ridgefield, then on to the Cape in the town of Westfleet, where we are now. We're moving again soon, and Momma's made me promise not to tell where we're going next. You'd think that having lived in so many places, we'd have met at least a few people who'd be able to see Lily, but in truth we have yet to meet anyone else who can see Lily, but I'm sure we will. Momma says they're out there somewhere and sooner or later we'll find them or they'll find us. It doesn't bother me anymore that people can't see Lily—that's just the way it is. It's like Momma says—everybody's somebody, but sometimes people aren't able to see it. Then again, sometimes they are.

That's just the way it is.